]

WO~~~~~ ~~~ ~~~~

Alvin Yapan is an author and a filmmaker. He is a fellow at the 2022 Writers Immersion and Cultural Exchange of Sing Lit Station and Royal Melbourne Institute of Technology University. His works, both in fiction and film, delve into the uncanny aspects of contemporary encounters with the non- and post-human. His first novel in the vernacular, *Ang Sandali ng mga Mata* (*This Moment of Eyes*, 2006), and his collection of short stories, *Sangkatauhan Sangkahayupan* (*Humanity Bestiary*, 2017), both received the Philippine National Book Award. His filmography includes *Ang Sayaw ng Dalawang Kaliwang Paa* (*The Dance of Two Left Feet*, 2011), and *Ang Panggagahasa kay Fe* (*The Rapture of Fe*, 2009), recognized as best digital feature films of the year in the Philippines and at the Cairo International Film Festival, respectively. He finds time to produce and direct films in the middle of his teaching commitments at the Department of Filipino, Ateneo de Manila University. He feels that his writing and filmmaking mutually reinforce each other.

Worship the Body

Alvin Yapan

Translated from Filipino by
Randy M. Bustamante

PENGUIN BOOKS
An imprint of Penguin Random House

PENGUIN BOOKS

Penguin Books is an imprint of the Penguin Random House group
of companies whose addresses can be found at
global.penguinrandomhouse.com

Published by Penguin Random House SEA Pte Ltd
40 Penjuru Lane, #03-12, Block 2
Singapore 609216

First published in Penguin Books by Penguin Random House SEA 2024

Copyright © Alvin Yapan 2024

10 9 8 7 6 5 4 3 2 1

ISBN 9789815204841

Typeset in Garamond by MAP Systems, Bengaluru, India

www.penguin.sg

Worship the body
Treat it with sanctity
Wrap and swaddle thick
In polyester silk

~

In the yard bury
And maybe in January
It will flower, fructify
In ginger and sapphire

—Rolando S. Tinio, 'Cantico Profano'

HISTORY ACCORDING TO JAIME

1

Drinking Glass

Every day, without fail, the newspaper arrives outside the door of Jaime's flat to report to him that the streets of Manila are truly the most dangerous in the world. Every time he opens the paper in the morning before going to work, someone is always being run over or sideswiped, a bus or car is crashing or keeling over. He is reminded that death is the result of the mixing of steel and sinew, of blood and gasoline spilt in the street. Though he is unaware, it has become a ritual for him to give thanks for every waking, having survived another day after the terrors of the night in Manila.

The accident happened when Jun put down the drinking glass with the ice he had asked for in front of him. He could've just gulped down the beer right from the bottle, like the other guys at the next table. But they were a brood of buddies over there while he was by himself. From his table for two, Jaime could hear their banter. They were all in long-sleeved shirts. They hadn't loosened their ties yet.

While he had already rolled back his sleeves up to the elbows. He had unbuttoned his shirt, revealing the white undershirt. They were probably employees like him. But much younger than him. Perhaps just out of college and only on their first jobs. Still looking for the job where they could settle down until they retired. While still searching, here they were having fun, shrugging off tiredness with their squad.

Their laughter reached his ears but he wasn't close enough to be bothered by it. After all, they were still young enough to not have suffered any losses in the world. Young people he had already interviewed a few times for his business. He was seated at a table for two because the restaurant couldn't find him a table for one. No matter how pricey, there was still no spot for a solo diner. The corners were full of plants and décor where he could have spent hours by himself. The bar had been suggested to him earlier. But he wanted a table. He was going to stay awhile. He was going to have beer even without company.

Indeed, in restaurants like this, Jaime had never seen a table for one. Places like this never allow any accidents to happen. All the movements of the employees are measured. From the guard who would open the door for him, to the head waiter who would direct him to his table, to the waiter who would attend to him. And so, it took a while for the accident to happen. He gave his order after taking his time perusing the menu, even though he had already decided he would only have a drink. He thought slowly, with the menu before him, as though he was waiting for he knew not what. Finally, the beer arrived and it was set in front of him. That was when he thought he needed a glass. He wouldn't drink the beer right out of the bottle. He wanted a ritual that evening.

He wasn't looking to get drunk. He couldn't get wasted because he was going to drive home. So, he asked for a glass. There was a ritual to the pouring of beer into the glass. Not like just quaffing it from the bottle.

That was when the accident happened. No glass shattered. No one slipped on the floor. No one threw up. No one choked. His eyes and the waiter's met. Just like that. In that orderly restaurant that didn't allow accidents, Jun's and Jamie's eyes met when Jun set before him the glass with ice in it because Jamie wanted a ritual that evening. He didn't expect that someone would join him in his ritual in that restaurant that had no table for one. That was when Jaime understood that around him, it had become rare for people to look each other in the eye.

2

Accident

So that was really Jun's job, Jaime would later discover. This was how Jun got a large part of his weekly earnings. Not from serving beer, not from setting tables, not from taking care of diners. But from creating accidents. Jaime's mother had died because an eight-wheeler truck lost control of its brakes and ploughed through the eight cars in front of it. But he didn't tell Jun any more about what happened to his mother. He simply paid the waiter more to sleep with him again the whole night. He didn't want to stay at his mother's wake that was full of people who followed so many rituals and superstitions that he ought to know—from receiving guests to not saying goodbye to them. He wanted to prepare himself for what was going to happen in the coming days. He knew it was only then that the series of accidents would happen, like ripples spreading from a pebble thrown into still waters. It was not his mother being pinned down by an eight-wheeler that was the true accident. Whenever someone gets run over in the streets of Manila, everyone still knows how to act. People still know who among them will cry, they know who will escape, who will call the police, call the ambulance, and who will stay to light a candle at the scene of death and wait to report it to the media. Jaime's mother being pinned beneath the truck was simply a pebble thrown into still waters. The real accident happened in the following days when Jaime confronted the empty place at the dinner table, the open door of his mother's room, the overturned plate on the table, the soaps and perfumes in the bathroom, the silence in the house that even his father couldn't stand so the old man drowned himself in work for their business since then.

It was meeting Jun that prepared him for everything that came afterwards. He first learned what an accident truly was when their eyes met. The moment they laid eyes on each other, he didn't know what role he was going to play. If he would avert his eyes or if he would return the look of the waiter who had brought the glass with ice. He couldn't say anything to Jun other than to ask for more ice to the point of having the ice bucket brought over to him. He asked for the menu again so he could order some more. He wanted anything that the cold beer would wash down his throat. Jun passed by his table a couple of times until the previous accident that was like the brushing of shoulder against shoulder in a crowded street turned into collisions in which things fall to the ground, books scatter around, wits scatter about, until what has been dropped is no longer only stuff that can be picked up but also breakable things like eyeglasses, wristwatches, mobile phones whose many shards all over the concrete street can't be put together again.

Until they are no longer only people bumping into each other but motorists careening at 220 kilometres per hour so they can swiftly and with utter abandon crash into each other, so the windshields and mirrors will shatter, so the car's metal will be crushed in the attempt to bring closer together the bodies of the casualties and those scathed by the accident.

All just because Jun smiled at him. It had become rare for Jaime to be smiled at by a stranger. And so, it was an accident when it happened. An accident that will rarely happen in a city where everyone already knows how they are to act.

3

City

When Jaime said that he liked the smell of Jun's sweat, the waiter simply smiled at him again. He said that Jun's sweat reminded him of freshly cut grass on mornings when he would wake up to the noise of the lawnmower being pushed by the gardener. He and Jun were lying side by side in bed in a hotel room then. They were both looking up at the mirrored ceiling. That was when he said that he had grown to love the scent of Jun's sweat. He said it to Jun's reflection in the mirror on the ceiling. It was also in the mirror that he saw Jun reciprocate with a grin.

That was not the first time someone had smiled at his comparisons. The one time, when he was in college, he was seated beside a young man. Every time his classmate would sit beside him, he would be reminded of the scent of pandesal. The morning rolls their maid would buy from the corner bakery. Steam would waft when the paper pouch was unwrapped. An aroma that would vanish quickly and couldn't be recovered by reheating or toasting. His seatmate was exactly that scent. The smell was not cloying. It was just right, like human body temperature. When he could no longer bear his curiosity, he asked his seatmate what perfume, cologne, or soap he used. He told the young man how his scent reminded him of steaming pandesal at breakfast. The young man sniffed himself. Jaime assured his classmate that the smell wasn't unpleasant at all. The young man replied that he didn't use any perfume. He smiled at Jaime then and stopped sitting beside him for the rest of the school term.

And so, with the next guys who caught his attention, Jaime no longer mentioned what they smelled like to him. Once, on a holiday trip to Baguio, he sat beside someone in the bus. The guy smelled like new tyres. He thought it might have been from the leather jacket the guy had on. Or maybe the leather knapsack. He and the man became chummy. They had a good chat throughout the ride. They met up again in one of the coffee shops along Session Road to continue the conversation. They discovered that they were both solo travellers up in Baguio and that they both had no fixed itinerary. They agreed to come up with a common plan. In all their plans, the one thing they did without fail was to have a drink when night fell in misty Baguio. But the whole time they were together in Baguio until they parted ways on EDSA back in Manila, Jaime never had the nerve to mention to the man he met and befriended on the bus that he reminded Jaime of the scent of new tyres. What he had told his parents then was that he was going up to Baguio with his buddies and they had a place to stay. He didn't tell them that he simply wanted to spend some time alone after college graduation. He didn't meet up with the man again. He never saw him on the bus again on any of his other trips to Baguio.

Even with the others he paid to have sex with, he no longer attempted to mention what they smelled like to him. There was one who smelled like permanent marker, and he wondered if the guy snorted drugs. Then there was the smell of a new pair of pants freshly out of the plastic wrapper. The scent insinuated itself up his nose, which he found intoxicating. There was the smell of iron, of aluminium steel, of laundry detergent. There was the smell of hospitals and of churches. There was the smell of a matchstick lit and extinguished right away. It was only with Jun that he had gathered up enough courage to mention what he was smelling. He didn't know why. Perhaps it was because of Jun's smile when he asked for a glass. A smile he wouldn't think badly of even were they never to meet again. It was at their second meeting that he mentioned to Jun how he reminded him of the scent of freshly cut grass.

It was as though he heard himself from faraway when he brought himself to mention it to Jun. He could now hear how silly he must have sounded. He could hear how, in trying to keep from telling anyone what he was smelling, he stumbled right away on doing it again after a while. He flubbed it because it was, after all, silly to liken Jun's sweat to freshly cut grass that would wake him in the morning. It would sound even more ridiculous if he were to mention the moon, the stars, the sea, the fields, and the flowers. But in everything he reads, when expressing fragrance, flowers always seem to be there, the aroma of morning, the aroma of dusk. As though there are no other smells in the world.

So that he wouldn't get laughed at the next time, Jaime thought of a scent to which he could compare Jun's sweat. He tried hard to recall how his nose had identified the smells of the first guys he had hired. That was when he noticed that in all the books he has read, no one has noticed the fragrance of a new car, the fragrance of a new movie theatre, the fragrance of gasoline spilled on the street. Not all of the city scents smell bad, after all. It's not all dust and smoke. It's not all just the smell of burning. It's not all the reek of rotting rubbish. There is an unusual fragrance to a newly opened book, the newspaper in the morning, passing by the bakery, and newly laid out carpets, newly crafted chairs in their furniture factory, and newly washed clothes from the laundrette. Not to mention all the perfumes sold in department stores and at the grocers.

That was when Jaime understood Jun's smile. It is only to women that one declares love using imagery from nature. If images of the city are ever to end up in the verses of the books he reads, it is a man that is to be the object of affection. Perhaps it's really like that, he thought once. Because it's always a woman who is being courted. This was what Jaime understood when Jun smiled at the comparison between his sweat and freshly cut grass in the morning. The city is a man. The city has a sheen. The city has a fragrance. There are the towering buildings, the linked concrete and hard road, the motion and energy of the machinery of the city.

Often, from the thirtieth floor of his office, he would peer down at the flow of street traffic through the glass wall. He would gaze at the cars the way others would gaze at the flow of water in a gentle river. Jaime would feel himself lightening up simply from looking at the passing of cars on the street. They would move with regularity like river-flow. To Jaime, rain in the forest is no different from rain in the city. It is still the same rain.

Same falling to the ground. Same sound made on impact. Same relief given. One time, when Jaime faced Jun's reflection in the ceiling mirror again, he knew what he was going to say. Jun's sweat didn't smell like freshly cut grass after all, but like gasoline that has still not been burned by the car's engine. When he said this to Jun, the guy beside him didn't grin any more. He saw that Jun brought his gaze down from the ceiling mirror to look at Jaime who was beside him in bed. When Jun looked at him, it was as though there was a light in his eyes the colour of lamps lit on the island in the middle of the street, of all the traffic lights, of the blinking lights of the disco, of the flash of fireworks. Not the light of the sun. Not the light of the moon that merely steals its glow from the sun.

Jaime loves the city because he knows the city. He knows the city right down to its nooks and crannies. This is where he grew up. His life and the city's are one. It's here in the city that his entire clan since their forebears grew up. It's here that his father sent him to school so he could manage their export furniture factory. He likes the feeling of how the city is the one that moves for him. How he feels like flying inside the lift. How he can move even without taking a single step. How it is the ground that does the walking instead of his feet.

There was a corner where one turned to get to their house. To Jaime that corner was like a gift. When he was still a child, this was where his father would rouse him whenever he fell asleep on the way home from school. There used to be a petrol station there. Before they got home, his father would stop by it so he wouldn't have to bother with it the next day.

While waiting for the petrol tank to fill up, his father would wake him. That would mean their house was already close by. One day, when they turned the corner, a twenty-four-hour convenience store stood where the petrol station used to be. He and his father would still stop by it now and then. They would buy grocery items his mother had forgotten to pick up at the grocer's and had relayed to them on the mobile phone. Jaime was delighted by those stops at the store. Whatever he would pick up from the shelves, his father wouldn't ask him to put back. He didn't know why his father had no will to resist him inside that corner store. The only reason he could think of was that they were already near their house. The next time they rounded the corner, the store was no longer there. Replaced by offices for dentists, solicitors, and architects. Then it became a laundrette, chemist's shop, and pet food store. Each time Jaime turned the corner, it was like unwrapping a gift again. And so, Jaime didn't feel any change, because although the car he was in was moving, the corner where he turned was the one that was truly moving, always changing. He couldn't really say that human life in the city goes by quickly. Life in the city doesn't pause the way everything stops inside a home. The city is like a home into which new furniture comes every day. Just as Jaime knew that every day his parents brought something new into their home.

The city is playing with him, Jaime feels. Playing hide and seek with him. Just like waking up with the feeling that there was something new in their house. Even when he was already helping out in his father's business, that feeling didn't go away every time something new was bought for the house: an earthen jar or even just drinking glasses, cushion, or figurines. All day, he would be restless until he discovered what was new in their house. When he was still very young, he wouldn't ask his parents or the maids. He would patiently scour the entire house, all the way to its nooks and crannies. It would be days before he would go to his parents or cheat by asking the maids. When he got older, he learned how to swallow his stubbornness and simply asked his parents right away. When his father and mother did notice that he had grown up, they themselves would inform him of what they had recently bought. That is how he feels about the city. Sometimes buildings go up in certain corners of the city that he rarely visits any more. Sometimes, just a fresh coat of paint. But in case he passes by, the buildings themselves, the parks, the posts, the billboards, the overpasses, flyovers, and roads introduce themselves to him. Though he doesn't notice, they are becoming fixtures of the city, making a home there alongside him. The entire city has turned into a giant gift that he gets to open every day.

4

Island

Indeed, he loves the city but every now and then he still has to leave it. Just as it is necessary to leave home sometime. That is common. Just as a lover wishes to be alone sometimes. Just as at times he gets up early, much earlier than Ria does so he can be by himself in the silence of the house even before starting the day's work. Yet the house remains a home to keep coming back to. In those times when he feels like leaving, it is always the sea that triggers the feeling. Not the sea that rushes to shore. Not the sea that drenches. But the sea of the silver screen. Whenever he sees the vastness of the sea at the cinema, whatever it is he is watching, he feels the urge to leave the city. An urge that is no different from building a house in the middle of fields or making a fan or a parasol amid the heat and humidity. So, not really the sea as a sea but the vastness of the sea. Jaime also feels this urge when he sees the vastness of fields on the screen even though there are thousands of soldiers killing each other there, even though the fields are littered with so many thousands of corpses, even though the expanse is made up of so many villages flattened by so many thousands of bombs. He feels it with any image of the skies where a spaceship is floating off who knows where in space. The vertiginous space is what urges him to leave the city of his home.

But it is also during such times that he feels the weight of what he needs to leave behind. There are his parents while they are still alive and have not left to him the running of their furniture factory. It feels heavy even though he has not many friends to abandon, other than the rare partner of his family in the furniture business, his friends from college, a few relatives: friends he seldom gets to talk to at business meetings, at reunions, at anniversaries, and a few special occasions. His special friends, Jaime calls them, although he does not see them regularly. A few more friends he added to his circle when he married Ria.

Still, it feels heavy to leave them behind. But every now and then the urge to soar grows stronger, to take risks because everything is starting to feel too small for Jaime. If he wants to get angry, he has to be content with heaving a deep sigh. It won't do to shout in the middle of the street. It won't do to bomb his office building. It won't do to punch what is making him angry. He has to make do with squeezing a soft ball. He has to let it out by belting out a song inside a small room. Or by hitting a ball. If he wants to show love he will have to do so through flowers, through chocolates, through balloons, through stolen delicate touches of restraint. Everything has shrunk so he wants breadth.

Someday, he will escape, thought Jaime. He will visit the island he once read about in the book written by Antonio de Morga. It was required reading for a course he didn't have to take. He signed up for it as an elective. His friends enrolled in courses on film or painting while he registered for a course in history. He was drawn to history even back then. He would profit off this course by searching for designs for furniture, for chairs and tables. But back then, he still didn't know that what was only a hobby would prove useful to him. He became engrossed with history when he discovered how the narratives of history were more astounding than the novels his college friends would read.

It is said that the conquistadores found an island en route to the Philippines. It was a Friday in July in the year 1595 when the Admiral Alvaro de Mendaña discovered a new island in the Marquesas. He named it Isla Magdalena, which the natives called Fatuhiwa. From the harbour, they were met by seventy dugouts, give or take, each one with three or more men rowing. The others swam toward them. Others straddled logs made to float on the saltwater. They numbered about four hundred men that the colonizers admired when they saw their physiques up close. Their bodies were erect, their muscles rippling. They were strong, handsome, with attractive teeth, eyes, lips, hands, and feet. Long golden hair cascaded over their shoulders. Among them were handsome young men who were completely naked, without a single article of clothing, save for some whose every inch of skin was tattooed. All that the colonizers could say to themselves was that the natives they were seeing had much to thank God for despite their lack of civilization, clothing, and intelligence.

And so, the colonizers were entranced when the men who came up to the ship invited them. The captain permitted the natives to climb aboard, and they saw how much taller the naked men were. They gave clothes to the natives, who danced for joy. In being so enamoured with the natives, it took a while before they noticed that the natives had begun stealing things from the ship. So, they had to fire their guns to scare off the natives who jumped away from the ship. The natives returned to their dugouts, throwing things at the ship and threatening to rain arrows on them. It was then that the captain's men fired more shots, which killed five or six of the natives they had been admiring just a while ago.

That is where Jaime plans to escape to, to that island where even the colonizers were charmed by the gorgeous physiques of the men. There on that island where the men were no different from the bewitching mermaids of Ulysses. There on that island full of Adonis-like Florantes of Balagtas. He will save up for his escape. When his father still hadn't passed away, he thought of working just as a cashier at McDonald's, Jollibee, or any other fast food chain. He wouldn't work for his father at the furniture factory because that would be like cheating on his escape. He should escape by his own sweat. He would sweep away other people's litter. He would put away their soiled dishes. Should he be ordered to clean toilets, he would do it. He would suffer everything he is made to do just so he could save up enough for his escape. He wouldn't deposit his money in the bank because his parents might trace it there, even if he opened a new account. He would stash his cash beneath the porn magazines in the secret compartment under his clothes. He would collect all his earnings there. He wouldn't worry that his money wouldn't earn any interest buried beneath the porn.

He would spend his savings but not to buy the plane ticket for Fatuhiwa. That wasn't what he would do. That wasn't what he was saving up for. Because he felt that it would be like cheating on his escape. He would spend it by buying a yacht in Mindanao. He would look on the internet for the cheapest yacht for sale in Mindanao. He would log on to the internet while his parents were asleep in the middle of the night. They would simply think he was studying. Once he had found a yacht, he would travel to Mindanao. He wouldn't spend any money on his trip. His savings would only be for buying the yacht. So, he would need to hitch a ride with vehicles headed to Mindanao. He would cross San Juanico Strait to get over to the Visayas, then take a ferry just to get to Mindanao. He would take risks on the road just to be able to leave Luzon. Even if he had to cling to the rear of jeepneys. Even if he had to dangle from the roofs of rickety buses with the produce and poultry, he would do it just to escape. Though people might cuss at him on the road, for sure someone would be bound to understand and give him a ride. It was in this way that he would get to Mindanao.

Once there, he would ask around for his internet contact who would sell him the cheapest yacht. He would inspect the yacht and he would take lessons for a few days on how to navigate it in the middle of the ocean. Then he would spend whatever was left on the food he would need for the voyage. He wouldn't tell the people there that he was leaving. He would just sail off one day. They would just wake up to find the yacht he had bought cheap no longer docked there.

He would sail across the vastness of the sea. He would shout with all his might. He would live completely naked on the yacht. He would drown himself in the vastness of the waters because he had been imprisoned too long in the smallness of things. Every now and then, dolphins and flying fish would glide alongside his yacht. Or it would be a flock of gulls in the sky above him. On these occasions, he would stop the engine of the yacht he had just bought. He would stop the engine so he could swim completely naked with the flying fish between the vast waters and the blue skies. He would swim in the company of dolphins until they took leave of him. He would keep company with them in their swimming even after the sun had set, no matter how many days they were still there with him. He would do all of those even when there was the threat of a storm or a whirlpool in the middle of the sea. He knew that the vastness would carry its own dangers. There would be the churning of the waters from squalls, a tornado in the middle of the sea, the thrashing gales. There would also be the threat of the sucking power of the water. But he would suffer it all just so he could escape. So he could escape the smallness of things.

And at the end of his voyage, there would be Fatuhiwa. Jaime could already see in his plans how he would reach Fatuhiwa. Perhaps the sails of his yacht would be torn up by then, some ropes cut off. Perhaps the windows would have shattered. Perhaps the paint would be scratched in many places. While inside he would have run out of food. Perhaps he would arrive in Fatuhiwa in a delirium from having run out of food and drink. Without his noticing, his yacht would simply run aground on the beach. Or perhaps he would suddenly hear shouts. Shouts he wouldn't understand. He would think them part of his delirium. He would think that even the shadow he saw leaping onto the deck of his yacht was part of his delirium. The shadow of a man naked save for a loincloth. The man would call out to his companions. They would all then leap onto the yacht. Men, all of them, just like in Morga's accounts. All of them well built. Their skin the colour of the wave-riders astride surfboards that he would see on the silver screen. An even brownness. Colour like his own skin from his adventures in the middle of the vastness of the sea, from swimming with dolphins and flying fish, from wrestling with tornadoes and whirlpools. And then the man who had seen him first would carry him. The man would have him sit up from lying prostrate on the floor of the yacht. He would lean him upon his comforting chest. Then he would give him a drink of the coolest water from a fragile glass to wake him from his own delirium.

When the accident happened between him and Jun, there was a little change in his escape plan. He plotted to bring Jun with him on his yacht and escape to Fatuhiwa. He wanted to see if the people of Fatuhiwa still had any recollection of the encounter chronicled by Morga. When the conquistadores and the natives didn't stick to the conventional script. He planned to take Jun there when they finally had the time. Perhaps he would take Jun with him on one of his trips to look for materials for the chairs to be made, to look for unusual and original designs, to look for inspiration, as his father had been gradually turning over to him the running of the business. In a few more years the entire business would be left to him.

But his plan to escape never came to be. He was only able to go to Fatuhiwa when he was already married. And so, after a long time of waiting, he discovered that the people of Fatuhiwa had no memory after all of the said story about the encounter between two groups of men from their history.

5

Ritual

And so, Jaime always wonders if it is really necessary for there to be no change in love, in loving, in admiration. When he and Jun are having sex, things keep changing. No repetitions. Everything is surprising. Sometimes it is the way a wet tongue brushes against a nipple. Sometimes it is a whisper, a groan, or a moan. Sometimes it is the caress of a thigh or the sniff of newly washed hair. Sometimes as quick as lightning. Sometimes lasting for how many hours. Sometimes it begins right there in the car, when the traffic light is red or even when it has turned green, when the vehicles in a row behind them are honking. Sometimes it happens all the way till goodbyes exchanged in the corridors of motels, amid the danger of being seen by others. Sometimes he is the one on top. He is the one who ravishes. He is the conqueror. He is the one being watched when Jun, who is beneath him, turns to face him. He is tongue, thighs, hands and arms, the cascading sweat, the mute and speechless. Sometimes he is the bottom.

He is the one who gives in. He is the one conquered. He is the one watching while on his back and savouring the feeling while face-down on the bed. He is the earth rained on by sweat and battered by flesh, but he is the one who can speak and is far from being mute. That is why between him and Jun, no one is really the conqueror or the conquered. Everything is according to the call of chance, the call of the desire of the flesh. Though he may hurt Jun while he is on top, he knows that there will come a time when he will be the one to feel the hurt. It is not just because he is paying Jun that he can do whatever he wants but because a time will come when he will be the bottom. With Jun, he can think only of himself, without thinking of anything else, let himself drift into the vastness of what he is feeling. In their copulation, he and Jun are equals until he hands over the fee or the next time he calls him for their next tryst.

He can't say the same with Ria. He always has the fear of hurting Ria. The first time they had sex was when they were already planning their wedding. They were exhausted from an entire day with their wedding consultant as they arranged the tables, the table settings, the guest list and seating plan. He didn't expect to be that tired from helping his fiancée plan the wedding. By then it had been a year since he had ended his trysts with Jun. He had decided that he wanted to start a family. His mother had been buried a few years by then. Only his father would be able to attend the wedding, along with a few relatives who happened to be on vacation in the Philippines. Most of them were already living abroad and had lost touch with them.

He dropped by Ria's house then to relax awhile before driving home to his flat. Her parents—his future in-laws—were not home. The maids said that they had gone to visit some wedding sponsors. Jaime could only sigh from exhaustion as he sat in the living room. Ria offered to give him a massage. Before long, they found themselves driving to Jaime's flat. It would be too awkward at Ria's house. Her parents might suddenly arrive. Soon enough he and Ria were naked in bed. They had left behind the dinner that the maids had prepared. In Jaime's mind, Ria had agreed to sex because she was sure that no matter what happened, he would marry her. The honeymoon would just come before that. It couldn't be branded a sin any more by the nuns who had taught Ria in school.

Ria was quiet in bed the entire time during sex. She just lay there as he undressed her. She didn't shift at all as he got up again to turn off the light that suddenly seemed too bright. The embrace of the young woman's legs and hands felt shy around his back. He also found it difficult, as did Ria. He should not not do it. That was how bodies were made for a man and a woman to encounter each other. He should not take it slowly with Ria. He was quick to understand that this was Ria's first time. He knew that this was still all new to his fiancée. Ria was perhaps feeling pain though she didn't show any sign of it. But neither could he speed it up. He couldn't get it out of his mind that Ria might be feeling pain and that she was trying to hide it from him. He didn't know what to do because he knew not which desire to give in to. He wanted to make Ria moan, but how could he know if it was not already a cry of pain. How many times had he heard that the first time is painful for the woman, how the man has to tear her virginity apart. And so, a ritual was needed so that neither he nor Ria would get hurt. Because if someone were to get hurt, Jaime would own it as a grievous sin. What was needed was the ritual of flowers, balloons, and chocolates, of stolen kisses and glances, of sweet terms of endearment, of dinners for two, of movie dates, of yeses and nos, of receivings and rejectings. What was needed was the ritual of getting to know Ria's friends, of courting her at her house, of asking her parents and relatives for her hand, of the processions to the altar, of the throwing of flowers and rice grains, of the kissing before all of humanity, of the yeses and the confirmation that there were no objections to the impending union. What was needed was the ritual of falling silent, the commemoration of dates and anniversaries, and of so many other firsts that should not be forgotten as a reminder that yes and forever will the sworn love not be forgotten.

Desire is selfish. He and Jun would always begin with orders. Sometimes it would come from him, when he was feeling bereft, feeling desire. At other times it would come from Jun: when he needed money. Whatever the case, one of them would always need something and the other one would have to give in. With Ria, it had to begin with asking for permission wordlessly, by feel. He had to gauge if he could ask his wife as soon as she welcomed him home from the office in the afternoon. He had to be able to sense if his wife wanted to ask him. For anything to happen with Ria, they both had to need it, they both had to give in. But they both know that in the sexual act, one of them is feeling more pleasure than the other. Always, the pleasure of one is not equal to the other's.

Desire is truly selfish. Jaime already knows that. But he couldn't shake off the disquiet in him, though he was already with Ria, though Ria was already his wife. The desire was coming from him, not evoked by others. He knew it because even though Jun was no longer there to tempt him, he felt desire. He knew it because even though he had stopped meeting Jun on account of being married to Ria, he still felt desire. He simply told Ria that he had sold the flat after they got married. He lied so he could have a place to go to every now and then when he wanted to be by himself. This made Jaime think that the desire for the city is no different: the self can never love it, as it is the very self that has made it.

6

Kite

If Jaime were to be asked how it all started, he would reply with another question. Why does everything have to have a beginning? Does everything really have a history? He had a happy childhood with his father. He suffered no cruelty at his hands. No lashing with the belt. No being screamed at. No beating. His father was ever at his side without giving him the feeling of being smothered. No shortcomings. As far as he knew.

One of the oldest memories of his childhood was being in his father's company. Once, he could no longer remember his age back then, only that he was not yet in grade school because by the time he started first grade, he already knew how to fly a kite. The memory of going out with his father was the one to teach him kite-flying. So, when they had a kite-flying activity in first grade, he proudly announced that he already knew how and that he would beat all of his classmates at flying kites.

It was at the seaside where his father took him to teach him kite-flying. It was there that his father took him not to teach him to swim but to fly a kite. His father said that it was good to fly a kite by the sea because of the brisk wind there: the point at which the sea, the earth, and the sky met. As he grew older and as he remembered this seaside vacation repeatedly, all the more did he become convinced that perhaps this was what had planted in him the love for vastness, the love for escape.

His mother was not with them then. Not because his parents had a fight. Not because his mother had a lover she had a tryst with and left his father in his company. Not because his parents had grown tired of each other. Not because they had conspired for his father to take him out on a father–son vacation. Not because his mother was ill and had to stay home. Not because she had work so she had no time to join them. Because he knew that he didn't look for his mother during their vacation. That a child has no worries is only proof of a deep understanding and trust that his mother is fine. Proof was the utter joy he felt in learning to fly a kite, for nothing was bothering his mind.

It is enough to say that his mother was not there for whatever reason that had nothing to do with her relationship to father and son. Because not every little thing was about them in his mother's life. His mother's life didn't centre on them. It is enough to say that on that day, his father took him to the shore to teach him to fly a kite because he wanted to, because he liked to. He took pleasure in teaching his son kite-flying just as his mother took pleasure in staying home for whatever reason. Perhaps when they returned home, his mother felt a twinge of envy at their kite-flying. But this jealousy would pass because she knew that she and her son would have their own time together without his father for whatever reason.

It was the rickety Ford Fiera they drove in, one of his father's first purchases from the furniture business. He didn't ask any more why it was that car they took. Because he was still a kid then, his attention was focused on the kite in the back of the Fiera where the chairs, tables, armchairs, rocking chairs, and other furniture were stored.

In his recollection, Jaime was certain his father didn't bring him to a private seaside resort. He was not able to ask his father any more before he died which beach he had taken him to. Because he knew that his father might have had no name to give. They simply took a right somewhere on the road when they saw a long stretch of dunes where they could run while flying a kite. If he asked his father for the name of the beach and he had no answer, he knew that he would feel embarrassed as though he had broken their agreement that it was not possible to give a name to secret joys. And so, it was not history itself but the secrets it harboured that Jaime learned to love as he grew older, secrets that sometimes were more startling than literature. That memory remained noble to Jaime until his father died and became more grand because he had lost all chances to name the shore where he was taught to fly a kite. As lofty and as noble as the soaring of the kite in the skies, in the blue expanse even though it was tethered to the ground as he and his father held on to the string.

His father didn't have a hard time flying the kite. The wind blew strong and steady on the beach. But even though he didn't run too far in the dunes to find the wind currents, Jaime remembered how his father had shouted like a child.

He could do nothing then but play his role as a child and holler along with his father as he flew the kite. There was a glint in his father's eye that he saw just then that he wouldn't forget. A glimmer that stayed alive amid the wind gusts around them. When his father let him hold the string, that was when he understood that the kite simply rode on the wind just like the human body riding the water's current when swimming. In holding the string, he felt the power of the wind and the greater power of the kite riding it. He then wondered what the kite felt as it flew in the power of space, and at that point, as Jaime remembers it, he fell in love with vastness.

7

Chair

He likes seeing Jun sitting in the chair he designed in their factory. He likes seeing Jun seated there without any clothes on.

He found the design during one of his vacations in France. It was the first time his father entrusted to him the designing of their furniture for manufacturing. His father already wanted to abandon rattan because it was getting harder to find a supplier of quality rattan. They wanted to diversify the carved wood line of their business. He roamed through the museums and palaces of Spain and France and he embellished what he saw in those palaces with a little variation so that it could be said to be theirs rather than just copies.

The product he designed was a hit in the market. More would come. They sourced the designs from original copies in the museums and palaces that have been around since the eighteenth century. In time, they would buy the designs of others to manufacture in their factory. At other times, they would be commissioned to do similar designs because they had become famous for it.

As their furniture designs sourced from the eighteenth century broadened, his first-ever design was still the closest to his heart. In his rented flat, that design was his room's ornamentation.

Which is why when he brought Jun to his room one day. Jun would have such an effect on the chair he had designed. Jun had dropped by his room many times. Even the guard had become used to him, assuming him to be a close friend of Jaime's. But he hadn't seen Jun seated on the chair without any clothes on. He had sat there a couple of times. Sometimes he would sit there after pulling on his pants and putting on socks and shoes. But he still hadn't seen him sitting there completely naked. Perhaps he hadn't seen the effect of Jun on the chair because his clothes were draped over the back of the chair. Or perhaps because it was Jun's body that was covered with the pants. He still hadn't seen the chair and Jun's body both uncovered.

It happened that time they were both already naked and the phone beside the chair rang. He stepped away from the bed to answer it. It was his mother calling. She was asking if he was going to drop in on them on Sunday. Since he got the flat, he would only go home on Saturdays and Sundays. But although this had become a ritual for him, it had also become a ritual for his mother to ask him if he was coming over. So that she could prepare the weekend meals, she said, because she was sure that he hadn't had a decent meal from eating out all the time.

While he was speaking with his mother, Jun followed him and sat on the chair he had designed near the phone. When he put down the phone, he was surprised by what he saw. Jun's body was there. Pressed against the planed and varnished wood. Even as he knew the flawless craftsmanship of the wood on which Jun was sitting, he still worried that a splinter might puncture Jun's skin as he sat naked on the chair. To his eyes the chair he designed looked hard. The kind of chair that queens sat in as they were taught the strict etiquette of sitting, eating, walking, only to be married off to a stranger for the sake of their family and kingdom. In Jaime's eyes, the curve of the carved backrest, the curve of the four carved legs and the armrest and handrest became hard designs. He learned that the curve of the overall design is but an illusion when seen from afar. But when a naked body is sitting upon it, it is stripped of this illusion as a reminder that it is still made of wood and not of cotton, not of clouds, not of angels' wings. Yet how is it that along with the realization that the curve of the design was but an illusion was the feeling in his eyes of how soft it was because of the similarly naked body sitting on it. He could clearly see how the curve of Jun's shoulder fit into the outline of the chair's backrest. He could feel how the centre of the backrest's design was tracing Jun's spine that divided his broad back, that he had gotten used to tracing and kissing.

And so, he could say nothing to Jun except to admit that the chair seemed softer because he was sitting in it. As though this was the most comfortable chair in the whole world. Which was why since then and whenever he had a chance, Jun would sit completely naked in the chair Jaime designed so its maker could watch him.

But it took a while before Jun got to sit in the chair. After the first night of the accident of the meeting of Jaime's and

Jun's eyes, after the first night when the drinking glass was set in front of Jaime, Jaime didn't return to the restaurant where Jun worked. Neither asked for the other's number. Jaime didn't ask Jun for his number because, to him, what happened was an accident after all. Even though this was not the first time he was going to hire a rent-boy. Sometimes in hotel lobbies, sometimes for out-call massages. Sometimes he would end up in go-go bars where rent-boys danced. And so he thought he would forget about his encounter with Jun. But after a few weeks, how was it that he was back in his corner where Jun worked, and Jun was his server once again? Before they parted that night, he was the one who asked for Jun's number. He would give him a call next time.

He didn't know what it was about Jun that had caught his eye. Jun was good-looking but just like so many other rent-boys. If anything, it was that Jun looked neat and tidy. He was fair-skinned though not a mestizo. He was not the typical rent-boy who would stand out if he were to be made to join a lineup in an aquarium. He was not a gym rat but took care of his body. It could be said that he had a swimmer's body. He couldn't see anything different in Jun but he knew that the accident he had created had already left a deep crack in him.

And so, one time Jamie asked Jun out to the cinema. He wanted to see how Jun would carry himself outside the restaurant and the hotels where he had taken him at first. He had Jun put on regular clothes that were not tight-fitting so as not to draw attention. They just met up outside the theatre. Inside the cinema, no grasping or groping happened between their hands. They watched the film because they were there to see a film. Their eyes didn't meet as they were both looking at the silver screen. And so after the film, they found themselves being attended to by another waiter as they talked, facing each other. And so after a couple more cinema dates, vacations in Tagaytay, trips to the rent-boy dance clubs, Jaime found himself bringing Jun to his flat.

He introduced Jun to the guard as his friend. They were not far apart in age after all. When he asked Jun how old he was, around twenty-four was the reply. But in time he would learn that he was actually pushing thirty. He said that age was an important asset in his line of work. His work accepted guys only up to a certain age. When your number wasn't in the calendar any more, the clients tended to move along. When Jun mentioned this to him, Jaime didn't get around to asking Jun what he would do after his age went past the calendar. And he didn't ask Jun anything personal any more since then.

But when Jaime saw Jun sitting naked in the chair he had designed, it entered his mind to ask Jun to work for him. He wanted to see Jun making chairs. Perhaps he could join the crew sanding the chairs. Or the painting crew. He couldn't be put in the woodcarving crew.

Jun declined when Jaime proposed his plan. Jaime understood Jun's refusal. Perhaps he didn't want an exclusive arrangement. Jun told him that sometimes it was frightening for rent-boys to agree to an exclusive arrangement with a client because they do not know what their owner would make them do. Perhaps Jun was aware that Jaime would eventually tire of him and the time would come when he would be let go.

And so, in the end, he felt an admiration for Jun. He admired him for having a life apart from Jaime. Because Jaime had gotten used to having his own life, it made him understand all the better that Jun already knew this about him even before he realized it. Not long after, Jun ended up sitting in the chair Jaime had made, Jaime's mother died in an accident. And after Jamie's wedding to Ria, his father followed his mother as though he had just been waiting for his son to settle down.

8

Stage

Their pretence was perfect whenever they were walking together amid other people. One would think they were just friends on a stroll like everyone else. About the same age. Chatting now and then. But everything vanished when it was time to pay.

When he had first asked how much he was supposed to pay, Jun declined to name a price. That is up to you, he told Jaime. He said he didn't put a price on himself. That made Jaime look closely at him. He told Jun that he had to set a fee that would be satisfactory to him. Jaime explained that if he were to pay him just a peso, would that be satisfactory. They finally agreed on two thousand pesos after a lengthy back and forth of hesitations and feigned nonchalance. Since then, that kind of bargaining never happened again. It was Jaime who set Jun's fee, more or less two thousand pesos. That was going to be their ballpark figure.

It was amusing for Jaime to see how the amount of money in one's hand controlled one's lust. Depending on how close to the two-thousand-peso mark Jaime paid, Jun performed his service accordingly. It became a game between him and Jun. Jun was pleased with the money paid to him when Jaime didn't ask him to do much. In turn, he was pleased with Jun whenever he paid him much less than two thousand pesos. Until he demanded less and less service from Jun and the money exchanged became less and less, too. The time came when Jaime's pleasure was not to be found in hotels any more. Sometimes he would bring Jun with him to the cinema or to the mall or wherever he was in the mood for.

Once, he met up with Jun at a mall. He didn't tell Jun he had no plan to go to a hotel. He just said that he had to buy some clothes first. He was trying to gather momentum to invite Jun over to his flat. So, they walked around in the mall first. Some of the stores were still closed. They passed by a row of monoblocs where the mass-goers would be sitting. It was Sunday morning. He suggested that they hear mass first while waiting for the stores to open.

While they were seated beside each other on the monoblocs during mass, he felt that they were up on the stage. As though they had roles they were playing. He felt something unusual. Not because he was heckling the priest that the hand he was holding while singing 'Our Father' was the same hand he was paying to get acquainted with his body. Jaime felt unusual because he knew it was all a farce. Jaime wished to speak up amid the crowd and admit that they were all up on the stage and watching each other. He was comfortable with this conscious pretence because somehow it made his work a lot lighter. He wouldn't have to convince himself that everything was not a sham.

Which is why it wasn't the pretence he was paying Jun for. He was paying the young man because he was becoming comfortable with their sham. Because both of them knew that they were merely pretending. Unlike the people around them: unaware that they were all only role-playing. When he asked Jun to go to mass with him, it was not to make fun of the people around him as they knelt in front of the host being raised. Not only so Jun would feel more at ease with him. He was preparing himself to bring Jun to his flat. He didn't want Jun to be taken aback by going to his home. The young man might scare off, thinking he was going to be made a kept man. Above all, he wanted to prepare himself to introduce Jun to the guard in his building.

So then it was not a matter of money that put an end to Jaime's trysts with Jun. It was not because of the fee. Not because of getting tired of pretending. Not because of the loss of the value of pretence. Also, not because of Jun's age. Not because he found someone much younger than Jun. Also not because of his mother's passing. If an accident was the reason for his first encounter with Jun, it was also an accident that caused his decision just to end it all. After all, accidents do not happen for no reason.

Jaime was heading home then. His mother had been dead for two years. He and Jun had just left the flat. Jun had just got off at the bus stop to wait for his ride home. As he made a turn at a street, a person crossing was suddenly caught in his headlights. Jaime hit the brakes. The wheels screeched against the asphalt. The air smelled of burned rubber. He locked eyes with the person crossing whom he almost hit. He who was inside the car, he couldn't believe that he managed not to hit someone, and for a few seconds the young man stood motionless from fear that he almost got hit. Only the windshield stood between their eyes that met. The windshield that was as clear as the glass that Jun had put ice in when they first met.

At the moment when their eyes met, it was not his mother who had been buried for two years that was on Jaime's mind. That perhaps this was what had happened to his mother. It was Jun who entered his mind. How even before the young man smiled at him in the restaurant that didn't allow any accident, Jun's eyes were no different from the eyes of the teenage boy he almost hit with his car, the teenage boy who was probably as handsome as those that the conquerors of Fatuhiwa saw. There was fear in the eyes of the teen. Stunned fear that he almost got hit because he was crossing the street at the same time that Jaime was turning the corner. And Jaime thought: if there was fear in the eyes of the teenage boy who didn't mean to get hit, how much more did Jun, who made a profession out of creating accidents, experience? He thought of the eyes of the kids at the pier who dive for coins tossed into the water, of the kids who run along the cliff's edge just to catch the airborne coins, of the kids playing hopscotch with train or bus on the highway just to win a bet.

Jaime remembered what his reason had been asking for a glass the first time he met Jun. He wanted to have a ritual. There was a ritual to pouring beer into a glass. Not like merely quaffing it from the bottle. There was nothing wrong with a ritual, especially for the solitary. Even the ongoing transformation of his beloved city was a ritual. Even the writing of the history of the island he wished to go to was a ritual. His trysts with Jun in his flat were already becoming a ritual. Even their sex was becoming a ritual. But Jaime understood that these couplings were only allowed within an order inimical to someone who lives by accidents.

He stopped seeing Jun in the days that followed. Not long after, he met Ria. He courted Ria with flowers, with whispers, with tempered expressions of love so that one day he would find himself waiting at the altar before people who were all seated with composure. Everyone knew the role they would be playing: who would cry, who would smile, who would read, who would light the candle, who would put on the veil and cord, who would sing, who would give them the blessing, when they would kiss, when they would applaud, when they would have their picture taken, when they would walk beneath the shower of rice grains in the hope that their destiny would be just as orderly.

Except that Jaime didn't understand that such order around him included the occurrence of accidents. Already part of the overall ritual of order are the accidents reported by the newspaper that he can no longer keep up with as they are delivered daily to his door. And so, when he gets into the back seat of his car one day and finds Jun behind the wheel as his new driver, he can do nothing but ask Jun how he has been doing.

HISTORY ACCORDING TO JUN

1

Skin

If Jun were to be asked how everything started, he would say it all began with pregnancy. Everything started from a series of misfortunes. Which could also bring about good luck. No one could tell. Because even the god of misfortune gets tired of bad luck every now and then.

There is a history to the colour of his skin. Even the contour of his jaw, the line of his brow, the swell of his cheeks. There is a history to his entire body. It began with pregnancy. There had been a married Spanish couple who could never get rich in Spain. When they won a game of monte, they suddenly found themselves aboard a galleon in Mexico, heading for the Philippines to try their luck there. And because of their Spanish blood, their indigo business prospered in the Philippines. Until, one day, a Chinese man happened to pass through the village where they lived. The Chinese man was peddling fabric of various colours that couldn't be produced at their indigo plantation. As a result, the indigo locals who had gotten used to buying colours from them experienced a shift in taste. They started looking for other colours among what their indigo plantation produced. The Spanish husband's masculinity was offended. A Chinese vagabond had put one over him in his own territory. The Spaniard felt the insult intensely, especially since he and his wife couldn't conceive a child. People around him were already whispering that he was sterile. In Spain, even, his sterility was linked to his poverty, which was why he ended up in the Philippines. In his anger, the Spaniard spread the slander that the Chinese man who sold rainbow-coloured fabrics was a faggot. Because he discovered that the Chinese man had come without a wife, as he crossed the sea on his rickety boat to escape hardship in China as well. If the two of them had come from a similar state of poverty in their respective homelands, the Spaniard's sole advantage over the Chinese man was the wife he had brought along. Faggot, the Chinese man who crossed the sea to the Philippines was a faggot! He was using his fellow men to satisfy his own lust. Not only other men but also children. Not only children but also young boys. He even used the cattle and goats. Not just cattle and goats but male cattle and goats! In repeating his spurious story over and over, the Spaniard managed to convince even himself that the Chinese man who sold different colours was a faggot indeed. Then he noticed that the Chinese man not only didn't bring a wife along; he also couldn't see any woman from China. All the Chinese people he saw were men. So even the other people believed the Spaniard. Chinese businesses were taxed exorbitantly. Until they were no longer trusted in the marketplace; they were even placed in a Parian, a ghetto, so that they couldn't infect the local indigos with their lust, according to their tormentors.

In his anger that the Spaniard's misfortune had been passed on to him, the Chinese man went up one night to the stone house of the Spanish couple who couldn't bear children. Because he could see no other solution to prove his manhood, for the Spaniard had all the power in the village, he raped the Spanish woman. From the Spaniard's wife's moans and groans beneath him, the Chinese man gradually convinced himself that he was indeed a man. And not just a man, his manhood was probably longer than that of the Spaniard. It was as though the Spanish woman under him was not used to such a thing. When she got pregnant, the Chinese man was all the more convinced that his was truly longer than the Spaniard's. It took only one try to get her pregnant instantly.

But, to the Spaniard, this was not enough proof of the Chinese man's masculinity. He had all the Chinese to be found in the Parian killed on the charge of sedition against the Spaniards. And so, even before news of the Spanish woman's pregnancy could spread, it was overshadowed by the grimmer massacre of all the Chinese incarcerated in Parian.

The Spaniard concealed his wife's pregnancy inside the stone house. One day, the dogs and cats found an infant on the street. The dogs howled and the cats meowed in search of the baby's parents. But none of their human masters admitted to who had given birth to it. When news of the newborn reached the rats, they took it in as their own. Because the rats had fantasies of having human blood in their veins. So that their kind could enjoy a little respect, they said. They had gotten sick of being hunted by cats and flogged by humans even at the mere sight of them. They only wanted to have a bit of stature in everyone's eyes. For the rats, caring for the orphaned infant was a wonderful opportunity, as they would someday marry it to one of their kind.

But what the rats hoped for in taking care of the infant never came to pass. When the baby came of age, what was seen was a human feeding among the rubbish, bathing in rainwater, hair matted with dirt, and unashamed of its nakedness. But everyone saw that the infant the rats had raised was still human. It couldn't be mistaken for a rat. There was nothing rodent-like about the infant save for its habits that were no different from that of rats. And that is why the rats decided that at the right time, the infant they had nurtured should have an offspring with their kind. Which all came to pass. The rats had no difficulty convincing their adopted child to marry another rat. The rats' adoptive son wed a female rat before a priest rat in a cathedral-like canal, though the Christian Church wouldn't recognize their marriage as valid.

The marriage of the rats' adopted child and the female rat bore fruit. Finally, the tiny infant birthed by the wife did look like a rat. It had a furry body. Only dirt made the adopted child's skin black. Now his child was truly black from the fine fur covering its body. It also had a sharp snout. The front teeth were large and tough. But only the race of rats believed in their own triumph. Because if they thought that they could sustain this explicit mixing of humans and rats, they were wrong.

When the son of the rats' adopted child grew up, he fell not for a fellow rat but for a female human. The first triumph of the rats in propagating a human–rat species turned out to be their last victory as well. From then on, they didn't attempt to create a human–rat. The legend of the wandering street vagrant remained the sole proof of this project of the rats.

But the foiling of the rats' plans was not that simple. When the human–rat and the young woman became well acquainted, he discovered that it was not a human he was infatuated with but a human–dove after all. He would have had a suspicion about this if he had only thought of where he had found her: in the house of doves in the convent's yard. And so the human–rat discovered that it was not love that he felt for the woman but the desire to eat her. Because everyone knows that rats eat doves alive, and this was why he had ended up in the doves' house in the first place. He was thoroughly convinced, or so he thought, that he was already renouncing his rodenthood for the love of the lass. He ended up proving all the more how his rodenthood was so much a part of his humanity.

The young woman–dove recounted to the young man–rat how, like his own history, she was also the offspring of an orphaned female infant that had been adopted by doves and married to another dove. She had been born as an egg that her human mother incubated for nine months, too. Her whole life she lived in that dove house. Every day the doves would bring them food so they wouldn't starve to death. When she once asked her mother what lay outside their house, her mother had no answer. She had never been out of the dove house because there were no stairs leading down. And she had no wings with which to fly out with the other doves. Her human mother simply told her that it was her grandparents who had put her up in the dove house. They failed to return to reclaim her because they both died in the Second World War. Her grandfather was a sensei while her grandmother was a Thomasite. They fell for each other but when the war broke out, they had to hide their relationship. So, they hid her in the dove house and she hadn't left it since. When she came of age, she wished right away to marry a dove so she could have a winged child to free her from the dove house.

She had felt sad upon hearing her human mother's story, said the young woman–dove to the young man–rat, because, when she cracked the egg that had nurtured her for nine months, she emerged without wings. The large eyes, the slender arms and legs were the only features she inherited from her dove–father. She inherited no wings.

That was when the human rat understood why the young woman–dove also loved him. Deep in the young woman's core still lay the dove-instinct that could sense the danger of his rodenthood. A danger that the lass already wanted to take on because she desired death in the face of killing her human mother's hope for a child with wings. The young man–rat didn't tell the young woman–dove any more what he understood. He kept everything a secret from everyone around: the rat clan, the race of doves, and the race of humans he encountered. One night he simply gnawed at one of the pillars of the dove house. Before morning came, the neighbourhood of the convent was startled awake by the crashing sound of the dove house that had been crushed to the ground. The doves flew in panic in all directions. Somehow, he helped the mother of the human–dove attain the freedom she wished for in giving birth to the woman he loved. The doves' adopted woman gave permission for her daughter to marry the young man–rat. The legend of the wandering, crazy woman of whom the children were terrified remains the proof of the doves' adoption of the child of the sensei and the Thomasite.

With the weight of the secret the young man-rat kept to himself, he married the young woman–dove in a church of the humans. He already wanted to forget everything; bury in his memory everything they had been through. He wanted to prove through their marriage that he could overcome the hunger he felt for his wife's doveness. He wanted to prove that his wife could overcome a dove's desire to die in his company. His whole life, the young man–rat took risks in the battle between belly and brain just to keep his family intact; especially when they had a son whom Jun would know as his grandfather.

So, when Jun was born, what became of his features came as no surprise. He had Spanish blood, which could be glimpsed in the shape of his face, the swell of his cheeks, and the cut of his jaw. It was hard to say if he had Oriental eyes because of the mixture of Chinese and Japanese blood in his veins; it was hard to see if his eyes curved upward or downward. It could also not be said that he was only fair-skinned because his Japanese and Chinese blood tempered his American blood. There was also his rat blood in the lushness of his hair and in having body hair at a young age. Even his doveness was there in the largeness of his eyes. In spite of the series of misfortunes Jun's clan had suffered throughout history, he became lucky eventually because the combination of different bloods in his veins was what made him a beautiful man. Perhaps because it was difficult to understand and trace which race gave him his features, people found him all the more charming. When Jun was asked if he would choose riches or good looks, he went for the latter. Whether it was a joke or not, Jun remembered the reason he gave his friends who had asked him. It was easy for someone with good looks to make money whereas it was hard for someone ugly with money to attain good looks. He remembered that they were taking a break from their game of hopscotch in the province when his friends asked him. They were lying down on the roof under the moonlight. Beside them was a pile of rubber tyres stolen from accidents on the highway in front of their houses all in a row.

Jun knew that no person would believe him if he told them his family history. So when Jaime asked him where he got his facial and bodily features from, he simply said what he always says to his other clients: that all he knew was that his ancestor was the illegitimate child of a friar.

2

Inside Out

Jun only noticed when they were already on the bus that he was wearing his T-shirt inside out. When he got off the bus with Oca, he also learned that it was not just his shirt but also his shorts that were inside out. He had truly been under the spell of his province for a long time. It had been a while since he had been imprisoned there; going in circles and unable to go out. He could confirm his enchantment only now that he had escaped, because of his mother's meddling in his clothes.

When he was the one putting away his clothes, he folded them inside out. He only turned them outside in when he was about to put them on. Perhaps he wanted to go against his mother's orders. She was always reminding him how to care for his belongings. How, when handwashing clothes, they should not be inside out when soaping them. And how, when rinsing, they should be inside out so that they can be that way when hung out to dry on the clothes line. His mother explained that if the clothes were to get sullied by dirt, dust, bird droppings, or sudden rain, it is not the side that others can see that would be sullied but the side that is hidden and pressed against the body. Even if they were to get sullied on the clothes line, they would still look clean to everyone else. Thus, when washing clothes, it is not important which side will be pressed against the skin. The only side that needs washing is the one that everyone else sees. Jun could understand his mother's explanations. But he also knew that his mother was merely following her own advice simply because she had gotten used to doing things a certain way. Not for any other reason.

Jun didn't know how he could be sure that his mother was truly like that. After all, it is difficult to live out a chore, a ritual, while repeatedly reminding oneself of the reasoning behind things. It is much easier to drift along with the motions, with chores, with rituals. And so, even though Jun knew the rightness of his mother's advice about organizing clothes, he still didn't follow it. His mother also meddled with his closet. His mother was still the one who washed Jun's clothes, which he seldom did. It was also Jun's mother who darned or stitched his clothes even before he found a seam that had come undone or a tear that needed mending before it grew bigger. And now, in his escape from their home in Concepcion, he had much to thank his mother's meddling for.

Because his mother had arranged his clothes the night before, when he put them on in the dark, he assumed they were still inside out as usual, so he turned it outside in. He put them on hurriedly. Oca was rushing him. He said that their bus was already leaving for Manila. No more time to say goodbye to his parents. He had to get dressed in the darkness of their house. He had to pack some clothes in the dark. He couldn't turn the lights on. It wouldn't do to rouse any of his housemates. So, when they got off the bus at the terminal in Manila, when he opened his bag after discovering that he had put his shirt and shorts on inside out, he saw that the clothes had been folded neatly.

Concepcion had some kind of power over his body. Whatever he did to escape from that place, there was always something that prevented him from doing so. He had just finished high school then. He was seventeen years old when he started making plans to leave Concepcion. He didn't want to be a labourer like his parents in the farmlands owned by other people. He didn't want to go with the trawls while waiting for harvest or planting seasons. He didn't want calluses to grow on his hands and feet. He didn't want his skin to burn from the heat of the sun or the salt of the sea. He didn't want dust to get into his eyes and make them tear. He didn't want to wear shirts with long sleeves, put on a broad-brimmed hat, and wrap his neck against the rice chaff that made the skin itch. Perhaps his escape from Concepcion was the urge to distance himself from the rat-blood coursing through his veins. Perhaps it was the dove-blood coursing through his veins that urged him to fly off somewhere and not be kept in one place.

No matter how much he saved up, Concepcion always created reasons to take away his money. Whenever he won at billiards, his mother would always fall ill. They would need to buy medicine or pay his father's debt from getting drunk at Mang Sebio's store. If not that then someone would get married or give birth or die among their friends or family so they would have to give a gift or make a donation. He had once made it to the bus. Suddenly a storm struck. All the trees fell on the street. Another time, an earthquake ripped

the concrete highway open. When a friend offered to set out
with him for Manila, the friend got murdered for, as it turned
out, getting a married woman pregnant. Though the murderer
was imprisoned, Jun was not able to leave Concepcion. And
when he decided to just go with a passing circus troupe, the
investors lost money so the troupe was disbanded.

So, when Oca had suddenly cajoled him, he didn't
hesitate to pack just a few of his clothes. It occurred to him
that Oca's sudden invitation might work, as he had never
tried to surprise Concepcion with a secret escape. Oca had
been to Manila a couple of times. But he kept returning and
returning to Concepcion. Oca told him that they would work
in Manila. Whatever job they could find: plumber, guard,
janitor, messenger. Maybe he would not be too picky when
it came to finding work, Oca wanted to make sure. It was
just going to be temporary, he said. They would save up first
so they could study nursing, PT, or even seafaring. It should
be at a somewhat reputable school. Not like the schools in
Concepcion. Just two years. After that, they would go abroad.
He said they would stay first where he used to live. Oca would
pay for the first three months of their rent. Jun would have to
borrow it from him while he was still looking for a job.

Oca already had it all figured out, but Jun was almost
hoping that something would happen to frustrate their plans.
He learned, as he sat in the bus, that a passenger had been
visited by a nightmare while waiting for the bus to depart
for Manila. As the driver waited so long for the bus to fill
up with passengers, that passenger fell asleep and had a bad
dream. He said the bus would be in a collision. They would all
die. He spread the word upon waking. The others had grim
visions. About five passengers decided not to go on the trip.

They didn't push through although they had already paid. Tickets were non-refundable, said the conductor. After much shouting and threats, the conductor still refused to return their money. They had not only jeopardized the trip but now also wanted the bus to lose income. Prospective passengers would be too scared to board the bus so it was only right not to return the fares of those who had gotten off. It so happened that Oca was friends with the bus driver. He had them occupy the freed-up seats so that those who had just gotten on and not witnessed the outburst of the passenger with the bad dream wouldn't ask questions. So, they had to rush their packing because the bus was about to take off to prevent more passengers from getting off. Fortunately, the bad dream of the one who had fallen asleep from waiting didn't come to pass and they made it to Manila alive. *Indeed, the misfortune of some becomes the good luck of others*, thought Jun. He had not only escaped from Concepcion but had also done so with a free ticket. He couldn't believe his good luck that night.

And so, when at last Jun found himself in Manila, the only thing he remembered that helped him leave Concepcion was the unintended reversal of his clothes because of his mother's meddling. As the old ones say, when you notice that you are lost going around in circles and can't get out of a place, you just need to take your clothes off and put them back on your body inside out.

3

Naked

Jun was still sleepy when he got off the bus. He fell asleep during the long ride. He had already put his shirt on the right way in the bus. On getting off, he noticed that his shorts were still inside out. He went to look for a loo. Good thing there was one in the bus station. He had to pay two pesos to get in. 'On my way out,' he told the one collecting. He was in a hurry, he reasoned. He asked Oca to wait for him. He told Oca what had happened. Oca laughed at him. Oca couldn't believe that Jun didn't notice how he had put on his shorts inside out. When he took off the shorts in the restroom, he discovered that even his briefs were inside out. The rain poured outside. Thunder and lightning. Gathering strength, the wind was whistling through the station's corridors. Suddenly there was a storm when Jun discovered that he had put on all his clothes, even his underwear, inside out. Jun wondered if there would still be a storm and heavy rain if he didn't see that he had put on his briefs inside out.

Oca was standing outside the loo. Waiting for him. Jun was still at the door when he saw the dust stirring as though it had been shaken loose by the sudden downpour. People were running to take cover. Even the stray dogs. Cartons left in the rain were crushed. Uncovered rubbish bins overflowed. The heat of the street reeked. Assaulted their noses. Jun saw how the sheet of rain gradually flew toward them. Like smoke approaching them. Before he knew it, Jun felt his whole body drenched. As though they had been licked by feral cats that meowed from being drenched by the rain. That was when he discovered that he hadn't only put his clothes on inside out— they were slowly vanishing from his body. Like smoke that was gone with the wind. Which is why his skin got wet, his whole body, in the spray. Gradually, as Jun stood outside the loo looking at the commotion the storm had precipitated, his clothes vanished. All because he had put on his briefs inside out. Even the bag he was clutching was becoming lighter because the clothes he had packed were also disappearing. Jun couldn't believe it. Perhaps he was still inside the bus, dreaming. But when the people around him started staring at him, including Oca who had stopped laughing, he became certain that he had already awakened from a dream. They were truly already in Manila. The man guarding the loo forgot to charge him the two pesos.

When even the briefs he had on finally vanished, the rain suddenly stopped. The sun suddenly shone. No more clothes worn inside out; the clothes that had caused the rain had all disappeared. Everyone squinted in the sudden blazing sunlight. Some put on shades. Umbrellas bloomed. The street began steaming again from the rainwater. No one was surprised by the sudden change in weather because they were all gawking at Jun who couldn't move and couldn't believe what was happening to him outside the loo. When Jun could no longer bear all the stares, including Oca's who slowly began to be ashamed of him, which was why he couldn't laugh any more, even before the cats could come out onto the street, even before the rainwater could dry up on the asphalt, Jun scrambled out of the station. He ran away from the honking of bus horns, from the barking of conductors looking for passengers on their trip, from the buying and selling of tickets. He went farther and farther away. But the dogs followed him. Chased after him like a burglar. His now-empty bag was still slung over his shoulder. He couldn't use it to cover his manhood because the dogs were at his heels and he had to scram. The dogs, who didn't recognize him, kept barking. He had no idea where to run to in his nakedness. Even the flip-flops he was wearing vanished. His feet burned from the asphalt. His legs darkened from the dirt of the city. The mud reached up to his thighs. The people he passed by stared at him. The dogs were still in pursuit. He had to find a place where he could hide temporarily. He ducked into an abandoned building. He needed to put some clothes on. What had happened to him was much worse than what had befallen his ancestor who had been raised by rats.

Jun climbed up to the second floor. The building had been gutted. There were only walls with paper postings; newspapers were scattered about along with a few sheets of plastic. He opened his bag right away. He was hoping that his clothes would have reappeared there. But when he opened the bag, he could see that the clothes his mother had carefully folded were no longer there. No more clothes he had saved up for in the province. They had all disappeared. His nakedness was absolute when he stepped onto the streets of Manila.

He heard voices upstairs, on the third floor. He hid behind a post so the residents there wouldn't see him. He didn't want to leave the building in such a condition any more. Perhaps the wild dogs were still waiting downstairs. He waited for night to spread over the city. He climbed up to the third floor. As expected, he saw some washed clothes hanging. A family of squatters was sleeping there. Two woven mats were laid out side by side on the floor. They were surrounded by sheets and pieces of carton and plywood that had been propped up. They were under a mosquito net because of so many mosquitoes. But not a single mosquito had any interest in sucking blood from Jun's naked body. Like they weren't seeing him at all. They only noticed Jun when he had already put on the clothes he had swiped. The clothes had been draped over the building's jalousies that had missing parts and the railing of the terrace of a small balcony. When Jun had put on the stolen clothes, the mosquitoes smelled his blood. It was now they who chased after Jun. They flew from their nests and egg-laying lair behind the abandoned building and from the puddles of rainwater on the roof.

And so just as Jun had entered the building in a sprint, he also sprinted away to evade the mosquitoes. Downstairs he ran into the dogs that had chased after him from the bus terminal. But they didn't mind Jun. He already had clothes on. They simply let the mosquitoes have their turn at chasing after Jun because that was the mosquitoes' duty in the city. It was no longer the task of dogs to chase after people within the city. Because in the city the dogs were already used to any and all sorts of people.

4

Revolt

It is amusing to think, then, that if nakedness was Jun's first experience in the city, it was a clothing shop in a mall where he would end up finding a job. He got in after Oca's acquaintances joked how he would make a good model for Penshoppe. So, he bought a fake Penshoppe T-shirt from the sidewalk. His friends made fun of him when he wore it. They said he was too gullible. When he learned that they were looking for applicants in one of the Penshoppe stores, he didn't hesitate. He just couldn't get a high position because he had only finished high school. He would be delivering inventory to sales clerks who dealt with customers. He was hidden in the stockroom and could only go out when they asked for stock that was not on display. He was not trusted to speak with customers and especially not with handling inventory. He was really only good for plucking stock that was at the very top of piles made high to save space in the stockroom. He would also help haul the stock from the garage downstairs to the stockroom of the store inside the mall itself. But even though Jun didn't engage with customers often, it was there in the stockroom that he understood the language of dressing up. He was able to deepen his understanding of how he really managed to leave Concepcion with the help of wearing clothes inside out.

He was truly lucky with his body. Though he didn't do anything to or with it, his body was beautiful. He was easy on the eyes. Despite being at the bottom of the pecking order at work and not enjoying the perks of free facials and a gym membership, he was able to maintain his good looks. That was when he realized that had it not been for his looks, he might not have gotten the job. He only finished high school, after all. Because he had a good physique, they decided to give him a try. Maybe he could be trained, said those who interviewed him. He had great luck indeed. From the inventory stockroom, he was eventually entrusted with customer interaction. Because one salesclerk didn't watch his weight and grew fat, he had to be taken out of customer service. It was not a good image for their business. They replaced him with Jun.

When the salesclerk named Efren and Jun happened to take lunch in the stockroom at the same time, the salesclerk told him how he couldn't help putting on weight. Even with a free gym membership, he still couldn't stop getting fat. When he used the gym was when he ended up growing stout. He went to the gym only because it was part of the work benefits. He was being considered for permanency as a cashier and the store's inventory officer. He would have been able to stop shuffling from store to store as a contractual employee. The Penshoppe manager was beginning to take a liking to him. But it was when they gave him the gym membership benefit that his unstoppable weight gain began. When he tried going on a diet, the rate of his weight gain doubled. He would skip a meal but he would only grow bigger. Like a balloon, he said. He didn't want to go back to being contractual. He was getting old. When he and Jun had lunch together, the salesclerk had only a slice of bread with no sandwich spread. It was Efren who told Jun how lucky he was to have inherited the body he had.

Jun was taught how to deal with customers. How to talk to customers who speak to him in English. Since presumably customers wouldn't talk to him except about clothing, the trainers made him memorize a few lines as in a stage play. The right reply for when the customer was looking for the right size and it was out of stock or when there was still one in stock or if it wouldn't fit. What to say to the customer who was asking if it was the right choice. And if there was something he couldn't understand, he just needed to refer the customer to another salesperson.

Jun studied how to deal with every customer. There were high-maintenance customers who needed to be followed to whatever corner of the store. Needed help with checking things out. There were customers who didn't wish to be bothered and preferred to go around on their own. He just needed to be close by so he could hear them when they made a choice. But not too close so that the customer wouldn't notice him and wouldn't feel insulted that he was suspecting them of shoplifting. Jun noticed that the first type of customer usually came overdressed while the second dressed simply. Sometimes just in shorts and sandals. Jun would just observe how each customer who entered was dressed and know how to deal with them.

The clothes were speaking to him, said Efren to Jun when they saw each other again. The clothes were persecuting him. He woke up in the middle of the night when the clothes he had on were strangling him. The snake printed on his shirt moved. Wrapped its tail around his neck. Efren told Jun he was sure that one of these days the snake on his shirt would already have venom in its fangs, and it would not only strangle but also bite him. When he went to buy a new T-shirt to wear, every shirt he touched spoke to him. There are no fat revolutionaries, said Che's head. Same thing was said by Mao's round face. He couldn't understand what the clothes were telling him. The birds pecked at him. The dragons were breathing fire on him while the shirts with no images kept shrinking and shrinking so he couldn't buy them. When he started to think he had been put under a spell, he went to a store selling religious clothes. But even there Christ scolded him because how could he be crucified if he was that fat. Efren didn't know any more how long the clothes he had bought before he grew fat could stand him. He knew that one of these days they would all revolt. He would be left with no clothes and he wouldn't be able to leave the house any more.

Jun could say nothing when he heard Efren's story. He knew all too well how it was to be stripped in the city. He had no advice for Efren. Jun understood all the better how lucky he had been on the day he was stripped at the bus station. When Efren couldn't come to work, he already knew the reason. He was not mistaken. The next day, news spread throughout the store that the neighbours had found Efren's corpse hanging from the ceiling. It was strange how all of his clothes seemed to have conspired to hang Efren from the ceiling. Because of his weight, the ceiling fan gave way and fell off. Through the resulting hole in the ceiling, the clothes reached out to grab onto the sturdy wooden beams of the house framework. All the clothes were scattered all over the room. But none of them covered Efren's body, which dangled completely naked.

One by one the clothes began to disappear from their store. Until the boss lost trust in the employees. The guard started frisking each of them on their way out. When Jun became one of the suspects, he thought that he needed to do something. He became vigilant. That was when he discovered that at noon when no one was in the stock room, Efren's ghost would appear. It would steal the clothes one by one. When he confronted Efren's ghost, it said that it was merely trying to help everyone in the store. The clothes might also kill them. When he died, he discovered that every night, when all the mall's stores had closed, in the middle of the guards' rounds, all the commodities in the mall conferred. Not just the clothes. Efren said he could do nothing except try to help the people a little. That was why he stole the clothes. Efren was keeping the people away from the clothes that were planning to revolt.

5

Restaurant

Jun resigned from the clothing store. When he was about to be promoted to sales clerk. Before he could be accused of stealing clothes. He couldn't tell the store manager who the culprit was. They wouldn't have believed him anyway. Neither would they have believed him if he would have told them the history of his body. He just couldn't fathom misfortune. Sometimes, someone's bad luck is also the bad luck of others. There was really no way to gauge when bad luck or good luck would come in his life. Even if misfortune gave birth to good fortune, it couldn't be said if the next offspring would be misfortune.

In his own way, Jun was able to save up a little money. Though it still was not enough to fund two years of studying seafaring, he enrolled anyway. He thought that if he was going to find work again, he wouldn't want to go back to the stockroom. He now needed a university diploma, or even just to reach uni, so that he could at least earn a better pay.

One needed capital to earn money, after all. He had already used his savings as capital to be a salesclerk.

Jun had difficulty finding a new job. He ended up being a waiter at the restaurant where he would meet Jaime. He had put in his biodata that he had work experience waiting tables. Before he became a salesclerk at Penshoppe, he had worked as a waiter in a small restaurant owned by an acquaintance of Oca's, where he was brought when he arrived in Manila. There were only eight tables in the restaurant that was not for the well-off. That was where he gained experience. When his former boss was contacted for reference, she had only good things to say about him.

Leticia was the name of his former boss. Leticia was married. To a taxi driver. Her husband's dream was to expand his fleet of taxi cabs. Leticia's husband was often out of the house, so she was the one left to run the restaurant. Jun discovered that Oca and Leticia were having an affair. When they lived in a rented room above the restaurant, they were given a discount as long as they helped with running the restaurant. Leticia also took a shine to him. But he didn't give in to her advances. It was not clear to Jun why his friend had brought him there. Perhaps Leticia was getting tired of Oca. Perhaps he was brought there so Oca wouldn't be evicted from the low-rent room.

Many of the restaurant's customers were taxi and tricycle drivers. Their dinners usually ended up as drinking sprees. They brought along women so they could flirt and sing there. It was there that Jun witnessed how a simple exchange of looks could lead to sex. Even Jun didn't escape the collision of looks in that restaurant. He joined in the fray of bodies, of thighs and legs, of hands and tongues. Inside the bathroom that reeked of urine. Inside a small taxi. Behind the restaurant. Inside the room while the snoring Oca was passed out from drunkenness in the bunk above his. Everything stopped when his friend begot a child. He said he had been ensnared by the woman. He only found out when he woke up one morning and she was there in bed beside him. He was told he had to answer for the woman. He said he had to go back to Concepcion. He would just raise his new family there. Jun remembered then that Oca hadn't worn his clothes inside out when they escaped from Concepcion.

Leticia wouldn't have asked him to leave. But Jun noticed that a couple of times, seemingly by mistake, she had walked in on him taking a shower. He looked for another place where he could manage to pay the monthly rent even on his own. That was when he had the good fortune of ending up in the clothing store. And now, he was a waiter at a restaurant that was far more beautiful than the business run by Leticia.

He was not surprised to discover in that ritzy restaurant the familiar meeting of glances between strangers that had been introduced to him at Leticia's restaurant. Jun told himself then that rich people were also horny, not just poor folk. His uniform now was the only thing different in this restaurant. He felt stifled by the clothes that they were ordered to button at the collar and button up even the sleeves. And so, it was no wonder that when Jaime called him over, Jun right away noticed his polo shirt with the unbuttoned collar and the sleeves rolled back.

6

Telephone

Undressing the one you are about to have sex with is a weighty undertaking. But Jun had no difficulty with Jaime, who was not his first client. There had been many others before him. Sometimes he would be brought to a hotel. Sometimes to their houses. Sometimes he would get picked up. Sometimes he would be told where to go for the rendezvous. Jun also knew that he was not Jaime's first either. He knew it when Jaime himself offered to be the one to undress him. Slowly. Piece by piece. His nakedness was revealed part by part. Piece by piece until his entire body was exposed. No rush. Restrained. Jaime carefully took off the clothes that Jun had carefully chosen for that day. The clothes that he had carefully washed and hung inside out to dry because there was no longer any mother who would preach to him about dos and don'ts.

Jun saw how Jaime was draping over the backrest of the bedside chair his clothes that were inside out. Like hanging them out to dry under the sun. So that later, afterwards, when he would put them back on, the side that others could see wouldn't be creased. Because Jun already understood that a person did not really dress for his body but for his surroundings.

He also liked seeing Jaime's naked body. Especially when Jaime answered the phone. Jaime got out of bed completely naked. There was nothing he could do but follow him. He sat in the wooden chair beside the table where the phone was. When Jaime pressed the receiver to his ear, Jun remembered how Jaime had first caught his eye. He saw in the hardness of the telephone pressed against the soft and fragile body of Jaime, his unbuttoned collar and the sleeves rolled back all the way to the elbows when they first met. While he was there in the wooden chair beside Jaime who was answering the phone, Jun needed to relive in his memory, summoning all the strength of his body, his justification for choosing to sell his services to his fellow men. He needed to remind himself that he didn't give a damn if another man paid for his services. It was very easy to say, after all, that his feelings wouldn't get involved.

7

Stitch

Six months—a year would have been long—was usually how long he stayed with a client before he became stale. When he was brought to the flat and introduced as a friend to the guard downstairs, he knew that Jaime was going to say goodbye to him soon. The T-shirt he was wearing then snagged on a protruding iron rod as he got off a jeepney. He was going to meet up with Jaime at 7-Eleven. Jaime had said they had someplace to go. Not the hotel. Not for a walk or to the cinema. The right sleeve of his T-shirt tore. It wasn't too big a tear, so Jaime wouldn't notice. The next morning, when he woke up beside Jaime, he got up immediately to see how big the tear was. He wished he didn't have to go home to his rented room. He was hoping he could go straight to work. He couldn't see any tear in the sleeve of his shirt. He thought that perhaps Jaime had sewn it while he was sleeping. But he couldn't see any sign of sewing.

That incident repeated itself a few more times before Jun began to suspect something was amiss. One time when two buttons popped out as he was hurrying to take off his polo shirt, the same thing happened. He woke up to find the two buttons sewn back on. When the underarm seam of his other shirt tore as he reached for the shoe that Jaime had hurled to the top of the closet, by the next morning it was as though the tear had never been there. When he fell to the floor from the bed and one of the seams in the crotch of his pants came undone, the same thing happened. Until, one day, when the rear pocket of his pants tore as Jaime suddenly pulled him from behind. He decided not to sleep that night and watch over how the tears in his clothes were being sewn back.

He placed the torn pants on the table near the bed. He was almost expecting a maid of Jaime's to come in in the middle of the night to arrange the whole room. Why it was like that he didn't know, and he intended to ask Jaime if he discovered that that was really what went on. But it was almost one in the morning and still no one came to open the door to Jaime's flat. Then he heard something moving on the table where he had placed the torn pants. He got up without waking Jaime who was sound asleep beside him.

When he was at the table, Jun discovered that it was the pair of pants that was making the sound he had heard. It was stitching the tear that Jaime had made. The threads of his denims were pulling themselves together. They were weaving into each other until the tear vanished. They didn't stop even when Jun saw them by the light of the lamp.

Jun didn't mention to Jaime what he had witnessed just the night before. Just as he didn't reveal the true history of his body. While Jun was putting on the self-sewing pants the next morning, he understood that, before long, he and Jaime would be saying their goodbyes. He never even got to ask what kind of job Jaime had, which funded their trysts, or even the last name of Jaime who, at three years and a half, had become his longest-lasting client.

8

Misfortune

Jun's suspicion was well-founded. Before long, his trysts with Jaime were few and far between. He had also taken on new clients with whom he would spend six months to one year, depending on how quickly they would tire of him. With any luck he might find another customer like Jaime who lasted three years and a half without making him do anything startling in bed. He had saved up enough money to finish putting himself through the two-year seafaring course, which stretched to five years for him. And so, with his misfortune, just as he was ready to leave the country and work abroad, turmoil broke out all over the world. In the Middle East, terrorists targeted Filipinos to force the government to eject all Filipinos living there. But he didn't want to become famous under those circumstances. He didn't want to become famous as a corpse. In Malaysia, Filipinos were being deported. All over the world, being an illegal alien had become more difficult because of tighter controls, even in the United States. Filipino entertainers were banned when he was about to leave for Japan. Jun felt as though the entire world was conspiring against him.

It was a good thing he met Maya as he went from employment agency to employment agency. After graduating, he left his job as a waiter because there was no career advancement for him there. He married Maya. Instead of paying an employment agency, they pooled their savings to buy a used car that, with the help of the husband of his former boss, Leticia, they turned into a taxi. He patterned his plans after those of Leticia's husband. He would begin with one taxi and grow it into a fleet. He would grow the business of being a taxi operator. He already knew that Leticia's husband was not able to fulfil his dreams because of his affairs with other women to match Leticia's affairs with other men. So, Jun would simply avoid having affairs with other women.

He didn't tell Maya any more about his former job in the ritzy restaurant. Every now and then, especially when a child was on the way, Jun would use his taxi for a sideline. He would also do it when the car needed yet another repair, as it was becoming rickety. He was growing old, yet he still didn't have enough savings to buy a second car. So, it made him doubt if Leticia's husband's philandering had been the real reason behind the stagnation of his business. One day, Jun parked their taxi in the garage and went to look for a job as a driver.

So it happened that, in an unexpected turn of events, when Jun went into the car that he had cleaned on his first day of work, he found Jaime in the mirror. He had heard of the job from a friend of Maya's who worked in a furniture factory, which he would learn was owned by Jaime. It was

Jaime's wife who had interviewed him. She said her husband needed a driver, especially since he had almost had an accident the previous week. Her husband was driving drunk; he couldn't say no to his business partners as they went around in Manila. Her husband would have preferred not to hire a driver so she took it upon herself to find one. Jun had to be good at his job so he wouldn't get fired on his first day. When Jaime's and Jun's eyes met in the car's rear-view mirror, Jun was not the first one to speak. He didn't know if Jaime still remembered him. He was startled that Jaime was asking how he had been. It took a while for him to reply because it had never happened that someone would ask him how his life had been, a life unspooling like a string of bad luck.

HUNCH ACCORDING TO RIA

1

Red

Anyone who says I'm not acquainted with change does not know me. That because I was raised in a school run by nuns, tethered to long skirts and incapable of cussing, not knowing how to let my hair down, I am unable to gaze at my own naked body. Change is etched into my body. I invented change. They say men and women age in the same way. Both witness the changes happening to their bodies. They are wrong. Perhaps, indeed, both men and women witness how hair sprouts from their bodies and how their bodies change shape, how their voices change. But everything happens gradually for men. So different from when I woke up one morning like any of the past mornings of my young life, except with wet panties. But it was blood I saw between my legs. That was the change. Startling. Not voice. Not hair. Not flesh. The experience of men is not like that. And now they say I'm the one who clings to things that do not change. To the big house where I live in a private subdivision. To delicate china. To silverware. To paintings hanging on the wall. To jewellery. To money and capital stored in banks and the stock market. To cars. To fine dining. To maids. To pieces of sculpture standing at every corner. To the lot on which the house sits. To clothes. To perfumes. To cosmetics. To my son. To my husband.

They do not know that I am change. Blood is change. I alone understand this. I understand why ancient people once mistook my body's monthly bleeding for a wound. The changes brought about by a wound and menstruation are equally weighty. Perhaps the latter is even weightier, because a wound can heal. Like when my finger bled as a knife sliced it while I was learning to cook. Like when my knee bled as I fell on the ground while I was learning to ride a bicycle. The changes they bring about are permanent and surprising. A change that brings fear and nervousness. A change that needs understanding. When Jaime and I first had sex, blood flowed. It was a few days before our wedding. Everyone was busy with preparations. I could no longer restrain the pulsing of blood in my veins. So, it was strange that I still got surprised even though I knew that blood would flow profusely while having sex with the man I was going to marry. I wanted to enjoy our honeymoon. All the fear and nervousness had to be dispelled even before we travelled abroad. I wanted no blood to be spilled on our honeymoon.

Change always comes with blood. When I gave birth to Francis, blood flowed. They had to cut me by a few centimetres. When his nose bled from too much heat, something changed. I awoke to the truth that he was no longer part of my body. He was no longer inside my womb. He had his own blood coursing through his body. I understood Jaime when his mother died in an accident. I understood when his father suffered a stroke. I understand the news about fathers and mothers having bullets rained down on them in the middle of the street. Destroying the windows of their cars. I understand the blood spilled in the homes of the massacred, of corpses stashed in garbage bins, tossed in some wilderness, thrown in the gutter. I understand even those who have drowned from the collision of ships out at sea, the explosion of airplanes in mid-air, of houses blown away amid a storm. I understand when the LRT blew up and bodies were mangled. I understand the shoot-outs in Mindanao. I understand how blood darkens when it dries, as dark as hatred and retribution. I understand the politics of nothingness brought about by EDSA because no blood was spilled after all.

Everything changed when Jaime and I first met. We met through the colour red. Red was the traffic light in the distance. All the cars with their red tail lights had stopped. Red was the car being driven by our driver. Like the red car being driven by Jaime that was right beside ours. There was a steady drizzle, and the red mudguards of our cars were getting wet. A tricycle and a bus had collided up ahead. Many were wounded. The surroundings were pulsing with the red lights of the ambulance that had its siren on. We waited a long time for the red light to disappear. I brought out my lipstick to freshen up for the party I was going to for a friend's birthday. That was when I felt someone's eyes on me. Jaime was looking as I was putting red on my lips. When I caught him staring, he smiled at me. I saw his smile amid all the redness, amid the pitter-patter of rain that obscured the windows separating us. When we had gone past the scene of the accident, I saw the blood washing off in the steady drizzle. A change had occurred. Jaime and I had already met.

I was no longer surprised when he was also there when I got to the birthday party. Neither our ages nor how we were getting older were things we first talked about. The accident on the street was our first exchange of words: how, in the middle of the traffic, it seemed as though more blood had spilled on the street. How life was full of accidents that brought along changes, which could never be adjudged good or bad for being new.

I can't blame myself. When Jaime had an accident, I suddenly forgot all that I knew about change. The car he was driving crashed into a post. He had been drinking. I just found him at the police station from where he had called to be picked up. He was not hurt or injured. No broken bones when we went to the hospital the next day. But someone had stolen from him, from the car. He had lost consciousness after hitting the post. Perhaps it was the thieves who had called the police after making sure he was not hurt and had just lost consciousness. So, there was confusion at the police station about who was to be charged and who was to be designated the victim. And so I forgot, I didn't notice, the meaning of no blood being spilled that night. I should have been able to connect everything to see it was nothing new any more. It had been going on awhile. It was because Jaime couldn't avoid drinking, it entered my mind then, especially when he was with clients and the supplier of the business.

Neither did I notice that I had been surprised to receive his call from the police station. I had been boasting that I knew what was going on with my loved ones no matter where they were. Even before they told me there was something wrong, I could already feel it. When Francis tripped in school and he cut his lip and had to be taken to the clinic, I felt something was wrong. I felt restless even though there were no changes in my grocery list. Hives sprouted on my arms, neck, and chest for no reason. I would wonder, then, when I was shocked by Jaime's accident; I didn't even sense it. When I could sense what time the moon and the sun shared the sky. I could sense, even without an alarm clock, what time to arise to prepare Francis's lunch box, what time to prepare Jaime's breakfast. I could sense when Jaime was going to be home late and wouldn't make it home in time for supper. I know when to take the pasta out of the water without pinching or biting it. I know when there is not enough salt, tanginess, or sweetness. I have a nose for such things. Etched into my body are the changes in the seasons, from the monsoons to summertime. I develop hives when it is summer and the weeds, the trees, and the grasses are hurling new life into the wind. Seeds with wings, seeds with tongues, seeds that can swim in the breeze because in the summer the wind turns watery and needs to be swum like the womb. My skin reddens from the explicit and unabashed copulation of plants just to get pregnant and bear fruit in the roiling of dust and the explosion of humidity in the intimate reunion of rain with the parched earth.

In my mind, my navel is an extension of my husband's and son's navels. I should be able to sense when their lives are in danger. If I'm aware of the world's timing, how much more aware will I be of the lives that are a continuation of mine? After Jaime's car accident, I revisited the subject of hiring a driver. A driver who would escort him to his meetings. Even just a company driver, not for the family. Jaime didn't like having someone else behind the wheel. I couldn't understand his initial objections. It was hard to drive in Manila. It was

tiring and it required the full attention of the one behind the
wheel. If he were to hire a driver, he could do more things
between meetings. He could rest or get himself ready before
facing those he needed to convince, those he needed to
silence. It entered my mind that it had something to do with
being behind the wheel that a man couldn't just give up. He
couldn't fathom how to entrust his life to a stranger.

But because he had just had the accident when I brought
up the subject of hiring a driver, Jaime didn't object vehemently.
He said he would try. I didn't like that kind of answer. I didn't
wait for him any more to look for a driver. He would forget
it, for sure. He would simply wait for enough time for my
argument to become weak. I asked around among our maids. It
so happened our laundry woman knew someone. A former taxi
driver. Married with two boys who were almost the same age
as Francis. Maya was the wife's name. Edgar was the firstborn
and Noel the younger one. I didn't think twice. I talked to him.
I explained the situation to Jun. That my husband would prefer
not to hire a driver. So he should not hope for a job yet. We
would try him out first. He should be careful with driving. My
husband needs someone to drive him home especially when a
meeting runs late and ends in drinks. We would park the car in
the garage at home. He would also take care of cleaning the car
and maintaining it when it needs repairs. But he had to inform
my husband first if he sees something that needs changing or
fixing. He should not touch the other cars in the garage. Jaime
personally looked after them. Only the company car was the
scope of his responsibility. I gave him a temporary mobile
phone so that he could be contacted easily about what time
and where to pick up and drop off, especially in an emergency.

The next day, I simply surprised Jaime at breakfast with
the news that I had already found him a driver. After a week,

we would decide if we would keep him. Jaime couldn't object. Even back then, I didn't sense that nothing changed around us. I didn't notice that I should have felt a change because a new person had entered our yard, our house. It was as though Jun had always already been there and been part of our house right from the start. So after a week, we didn't let go of Jun. Sometimes he was not just a company driver. I would also call him to drive for me and Francis. He would also drive the company's delivery truck. Jun would also borrow our car and park it in his garage at home. It should have surprised me when I discovered that he was also already the one looking after Jaime's other cars in the garage.

I only sensed something when Jaime brought some roses home for me. There was no special occasion, but he brought roses. It was not anyone's birthday in the family. It was not our anniversary. There was nothing to celebrate or commemorate. He brought home roses that were spreading redness everywhere. Redness that reminded me of accidents, of blood, of changes, of the knowledge I had temporarily forgotten. I sensed no change in what was expected to change or a change in what was expected to remain unchanged. I could no longer figure out then which of the two I really sensed: a change or no change? And so, what was change after all? I asked myself upon whose body change had been etched. Did I feel the change because of the roses he had brought or because the roses he brought were red? If he had brought a different colour of roses, would I not have felt any change? Would it have been better if he had brought a different colour of roses? I could no longer point out which of the two was the problem: the roses or the colour red.

2

Water

No blood was spilled when I discovered what was happening between Jaime and Jun. It was tears that flowed, clear as the water from the tap for washing the dishes, washing dirt from the body. Like the water from the hose for watering the plants. Clear as rainwater that becomes midwife to hundreds of lives scattered all over the parched earth. Not tears from an outburst that ends up in swollen eyes and interrogation. The tears of unexplainable sobbing done secretly. Or perhaps tears of shock. But I'm certain they are still as salty as the sea where the body rests in the heat of summer, where many kinds of fish swim: all colours and shapes, wild or tame, whale and jellyfish, dolphin and flying fish, rainbow corals. How beautifully they swim in the salt of the sea. There is an unusual grace in the flapping of their tiny fins, the waving of their tails as they sluice through the water between corals, even in their splatter.

Though our hands and feet are ungainly in the water, we still try to mimic the fish. Because it is with movements that we fall in love. It is movements I fall in love with. With the wave of a hand, an unusual gait, a way of looking, the furrowing of the forehead, how one sits in a chair, how one writes, how one lays one's head on a pillow, how one closes one's eyes while asleep, and how one yawns in the morning. How one sneezes and hiccups. Bursts out in laughter. Smiles. Pleads. Shows affection. Inquires. And so, I discovered everything without the help of doors left ajar, left unlocked. No sudden homecoming. No names called out while dreaming. No rebuffed kisses. No moaning walls. No suspicions and snoopings. No smells clinging to clothes. It was in the movements. In small things. Because I understand that it is not with the big things encompassing the universe that we fall in love. It is with the kisses. With the whispers. With the holding and caressing of the hand. With the leaning against the chest. It is with such things.

Jaime came home drunk once. I woke up from the maid's knock on our bedroom door. She said my husband was in the living room. Jun had him lie down on the sofa. When I got downstairs, Jun explained that Jaime and his clients seemed to have had a drinking spree. That didn't surprise me. It was for times like these that we hired Jun as a driver. Jun apologized as though it was his fault. He said he didn't know that Jaime was going to get that wasted. Before he knew it, Jaime had been helped by his two business partners into the car where he had been waiting. Jaime had thrown up in the back of the car. 'Do not worry,' I told Jun, this happens just once in a while. Just a few times a year. Only when he gets together again with his clients.

I asked Jun to help me carry Jaime upstairs to the bedroom. He was by the right shoulder while I was by the left. Because of Jaime's weight, I knew that Jun was trying hard to carry all of my husband's weight. He didn't want me to have a hard time doing it, especially going up the stairs. We almost had to throw Jaime down onto the bed. The maid followed us into the room. She had brought warm water and a washcloth. She gave the basin to Jun and stood by the door to wait to replace the water. Jun helped me prop Jaime up in bed so we could take his polo shirt off. I couldn't tell Jun that I'd take care of it. I knew that I couldn't carry Jaime by myself. Perhaps Jun noticed how my nose wrinkled upon seeing the vomit that clung to the polo shirt's collar. Jun said he would be the one to wipe the vomit from Jaime's cheeks and neck. He said he would take care of it first, before the vomit in the back seat of the car. He even managed to crack a joke. He said he would leave with the maid later who was watching them from the doorway. I didn't object any more. I started taking off Jaime's shoes. From the foot of the bed, I saw how Jun wiped Jaime's cheeks and neck. He seemed very familiar with my husband's body. That was when I discovered that the sacredness of a place does not depend on it remaining a secret. Sacred was the groove behind my husband's ear, the groove where I'd put my tongue, my finger as our bodies made love. That was my secret nook in Jaime's body, if a lover's body could be called a home. When Jun touched it, without having to guide his hands with his eyes, I thought that it was no different from the way a gardener cradles a bud about to bloom at dawn. No different from the way the bodies of fish slice through the salt of the sea. No different from caressing a scar in remembrance of a wound.

My eyes opened to the hands of Jaime and Jun. They were no different from larks, kingfishers, and herons in their flirtations with the earth as they fly. They soar away from the earth and do not descend from the skies for a spell. Every time Jaime and Jun were close to each other, their hands were like birds swooping into each other's path. Their skins never touch. There was the passing of glasses, of cutlery, of bags without even the tips of their fingers touching. But I knew, even from afar, even when I was just observing them, that they knew each other's bloodbeat just as the bird knows the world's tug. Their fingers were merely sending out feelers. The waft of body heat was enough to be assured of each other's presence before leaving again like a bird soaring skyward. Even Jun's eyes were birds when he looked at Jaime. Jaime once asked Jun if his clothes looked fine. We were going to a party then. A friend's wedding anniversary. When we got out of the car, Jaime turned to face Jun and asked if his clothes didn't look bad. I was holding Jaime's hand to feel how he reddened, when Jun looked him over, when Jun's gaze examined his entire body from head to toe.

But I only noticed all of that because that was also how Jaime would hold my hand. That was how his hand felt when he had his hand on my waist from behind. He was like that when he whispered. That was how he looked at me when he gave me the red roses. I also knew how to become now-earth, now-water, hot and cold beneath his winged palms. I knew how his eyes made a map of my body. Oh, how light the birds are in flight but how heavy, too, because they will surely come down to earth! That indeed is how the bird plays with the earth in riding the wave of wind in the air. At the same time, I could almost see how Jun became water beneath

Jaime's body, became heavy now, then became light on top of him. Jun became water, a vast sea called to by Jaime's wings. He became a harsh sea in the rise and fall of his wild waves. He also became a tranquil creek, a glass surface for Jaime's own body to mirror as it flew like a kite. A kite holding on to the string of a lover's body, of a mate.

In the meantime, I kept to myself what I had discovered between Jaime and Jun. I do not know why. Perhaps because what I discovered didn't come out of big things. They were only small matters. I couldn't trust my intuition, which, as things were, no longer knew how to separate roses from the colour red. It is humbling to know that I can't possess the power of becoming earth and water beneath a beloved. I can't possess even the courage of a bird to fly off into the vastness. No one person can possess such powers.

3

Burnay

Francis broke the earthen vessel I had bought all the way in Vigan. Jaime and I were touring the provinces back then to look for large earthenware that would ornament the furniture display centres, which I managed. Jaime didn't prevent me from helping out with his business even though I didn't really need to work for our family. I already had stock investments even before Jaime and I got married. My parents' gift to me. I just get a call in case I wish to sell. I have advisers even in these decision-making matters so it is not difficult. It just takes guts. Like in gambling.

The furniture factory's earnings were sufficient. It was running on its own. What needed to be overseen was changing the designs, the streamlining the crafting of furniture from fragments, looking after the workers, especially the carvers, so they wouldn't leave, searching for new suppliers in case they were needed for a new design or if the former supplier was affected by things like a log ban or the decline in the quality of rattan. It was only such things that Jaime oversaw.

I had no place there, so I was simply given the management of the display centre. I also managed our participation in trade fairs and furniture exhibits. If Jaime was in charge of running the factory, I was the one responsible for promoting our products to the whole country. Jaime's business used to run solely on the strength of having foreign buyers. If they had any advertising back then, it was only trade fairs and newspapers that would direct the customer to the one display outlet near the factory. Because foreign bulk orders were clearly more profitable, that was Jaime's focus. I told him that there was nothing wrong with my managing our local display centre. 'Long-term investment,' I said. The day would come when his foreign customers would find another supplier that he wouldn't be able to match. Even now, we already needed to strengthen our brand in the local market; even if it was just an occasional customer, they could be counted on in the future. I added that there was a construction boom in the country that would need a supplier of furniture.

Jaime didn't object to my help in the business. I gained a job outside of managing the house. Perhaps he was aware that I needed to work after going to college and obtaining a degree in business administration. What a waste not to use it, Jaime understood. He even helped me scour Vigan to look for makers of earthenware that would complete the interior design of our Filipiniana outlets. The Ilocanos call their earthenware burnay. I bought a number of giant earthen vessels for the store I was going to manage. As a gift, the vendor gave me a vessel with an unusual shape. Whenever the body of the vessel they were making would collapse on the wheel of the factory, resulting in unusual shapes, they would go on moulding it and eventually sell it. There were many buyers of such vessels. It was unusual that many found these vessels that were moulded with their imperfection beautiful. I placed the burnay in one of the corners of the living room. The burnay has been there in the corner since we started living in Jaime's house. It hasn't been moved as though it was already in its rightful place even before it was made. It was there as a reminder of Jaime's help in getting me started on managing the display centres of his furniture. It was only when Francis broke the burnay while playing ball in the house that I noticed how beautiful the burnay that had been given to me as a gift by the vendor from whom we had bought earthenware really was. It was only such things that could be given as a gift. But I only realized it when it got shattered.

4

Clothing

It is truly like this for everyone who has broken something. It always comes with self-blame. One for the person who did the breaking, which is easy to understand. He is the one who incurs ire and is scolded. He is the one screamed at. But he is also the one who is consoled eventually, told that he should not feel too bad because he didn't really mean to. It is not like that for someone else who is self-blaming. I blamed myself when Francis broke the burnay. I was the reason the burnay had been placed there. Why was it there in the corner where my son's ball would hit it? Of all the corners of the house, what made me think of having the burnay, which is a reminder of Jaime's approval of my helping out in his business, placed there? So, it is no longer easy to tell oneself that memory is more important than the thing that guards it. I became all the more certain that it is difficult to guard memories that slip from the mind like a hand holding water, so there are things that serve as their sentinel.

When I discovered what was going on between Jaime and Jun based on small things, I came up with a plan. When I had already put up a number of our display centres in the malls of SM, Greenhills, and Glorietta, I'd just go from store to store with nothing to do. There were few walk-in customers in furniture display centres. It was lonely to sit amid so many vacant chairs and tables no matter how beautifully etched they were. Sometimes I think that I'm haunted from having my eyes invent people sitting in them.

This was where I asked Jun to come after he had dropped off Francis and Jaime at school and the office. I told him I needed help carrying things I was going to buy. My plan was simple. I just wanted to get to know the man whom I glimpsed in the little changes in Jaime—in the way he held me, the way he looked at me. I blamed myself for being the reason why they met. I wanted to scold him like the notice posted in the store: anything you break is already yours and you need to pay for it.

I took Jun with me as I shopped for clothes. I had him carry the bags. Normally I would not have made him do it. Everyone at home knew that I could shop for clothes or groceries by myself, unaided. I made sure that as we went from store to store, I never walked ahead of Jun. I walked right beside him as though we were a married couple. I wanted to tease him until he knelt at my feet. I tried on a top. I called him over to the fitting room. I opened the door and asked him just like my husband would ask him if he looked fine in his clothes. I was searching in Jun's gaze, for the look he gave my husband from head to toe. I was searching in Jun's eyes for the way my husband looked at me now. But I could find nothing in Jun's eyes. He said he didn't know how to look at women's clothes. He couldn't look at me. I asked him if he didn't have a wife, as though I didn't already know when he had first worked for us. That was when he looked at me. He replied that he did have a wife. Her name was Maya, and they already had two young boys both studying in grade school like my son Francis.

One day, my employees at the display centre and I had been talking about other stores that purposely place their fragile merchandise in precarious and narrow corridors where customers pass so that they could sell them. We were arranging the store then. We were trying to figure out how to vary the store's look. To ease our boredom with the unchanging look of the store every day, we rearranged the store not for the customers but for lack of something to occupy ourselves with. When Jun dropped me off at home from clothes shopping, I glanced at our house from the outside. Jun drove the car very slowly into the garage. It was only then, again, that I was able to study how our house looked and I saw that the house I shared with Jaime and Francis was a home, not a store.

5

By the Sea

I woke up in the morning without help from the alarm clock. The food we would be bringing to the beach needed to be prepared. The night before, I had prepared our clothes, including the bags for the things that would get wet. I had already packed the sunblock and the first aid kit. It would be Francis's first time swimming in the sea. It was our first beach excursion as a family. It had never occurred to Jaime and me to take Francis to the beach. Usually, for vacation, we would travel abroad. We would take him to different foreign places. But it had never crossed our mind to take him to the sea wherever we went. Even though Francis had hinted several times that he wanted to see the ocean. Jaime and I never allowed him to join any field trip that would drive by the sea. If we ever allowed him to swim, it would only be in the swimming pool. Perhaps we were afraid of Francis being near the sea. The waves were treacherous. The tides behaved differently below the surface. To the human body, it felt different to swim in the salt of the secretive swaying of the surf.

Yet truly everything changes. Jaime surprised me the past week. He asked if I would like us to take Francis to the sea. He said Jun would drive us there. Jun would also bring along his two sons and Maya. Jun knew a beach in Batangas where the water was not too deep for the children. We wouldn't have to cross the sea just to find a place to swim. We would just take the car. Be back home in the afternoon. We would just have to prepare some food to bring along in case someone got hungry. We could have our lunch cooked over there. When Francis heard of his father's plan, I couldn't object because of his utter glee. He already wanted us to buy him goggles, flippers, and all swimming accessories although he didn't even know how to float yet.

Jun arrived with his family in the office car. We were going to take the SUV for the trip. I asked Jun, Maya, Edgar, and Noel to come into the house first since the maid hadn't finished making the sandwiches for the road. I told them not to be shy. Jun's boys were not frisky. Edgar was about seven years old, like Francis. Noel was only about a year or two younger than his brother. They just sat on the sofa. Perhaps their mother had threatened to leave them behind if they misbehaved. Jun went out to the garage to get the SUV ready. Maya and I were left to ourselves. We exchanged how-are-yous. Both hoped it wouldn't rain. Both complained about how hard it was to rouse our husbands and boys from sleep. We felt awkward about each other. When Francis came down, he was already wearing his snorkelling outfit. I introduced him to Maya and Jun's boys. The children just looked at each other. I looked over at Maya. I didn't know if she knew what was really happening. There we were, with Jaime and Jun putting even our kids side by side. They were being made to stand side by side by our husbands, not just us. Comparing them.

So that was what happened all day. I doubted what I had read in the changes I had seen in Jaime. Perhaps there was really nothing between him and Jun. Perhaps it was only in my imagination. When Jaime came down and we were heading out, he asked Jun if he could manage to drive all the way to Batangas without Jaime taking over the wheel. Yes, said Jun immediately, like he was accepting a challenge. Jaime insisted that they could take turns driving. The argument ended when Jun mentioned that Batangas had not been the longest drive on his own, when he was still driving a taxi. He made it to Nueva Ecija. He made it to Bicol. Jaime sat beside Jun in the front seat. We sat the kids in the rear seats. Maya and I sat in the middle row. Even Francis behaved when Maya warned her boys that they would get thrown out the window if they became pesky. So the trip was peaceful. Jun and Jaime argued again when it was time to stop at a petrol station. They argued about who knew more when it came to who provided better service, who the petrol cartels were. In all their back and forth, I didn't notice where we did end up getting petrol. As for Maya and me, we were almost running out of things to discuss, from the weather to our kids and the difficulty of raising children.

In bringing down our things from the vehicle, it looked as though Jun and Jaime were in a lifting contest. Jaime had a gym in our house so he wouldn't let Jun beat him. He almost grabbed the Coleman that was full of our drinking water. We just brought our own so we wouldn't have to buy it there, because we had children with us. When Jaime felt the strain

of lifting and momentarily put the Coleman down on the
sand, Jun picked it up right away and carried it to our rented
resort. Panting, Jaime didn't protest. At the resort, Jaime
refused the cash contribution Jun offered for the rental. Our
resort came with a hut on the beach. Maya simply looked at
me. She shyly gave thanks for letting them come along, which
in turn made me feel shy toward her. I told Maya that had
they not come along, Jaime and I might not have gone there
at all. It would be so boring if we were the only family there.
Francis was an only child. No playmates. So, I should be the
one to say thanks. 'Don't we have other families to invite?'
quipped Maya. Which made me feel all the more ashamed for
the doubts playing in my head about Jaime and Jun. I wish I
could speak with Maya about our husbands. I just told Maya
not to be embarrassed any more because men were really
like that. Always wanting to prove who could shoot their pee
farther. Always competing. I added that they might already
be using our sons in their contest. That was when Maya
smiled. She said she had noticed even back at the house. We
shared a laugh and started discussing the competition we
noticed between our husbands. Maya and I finally grew at
ease with each other. I found myself very much immersed in
exchanging stories with Maya.

'My boys look like they broke out of jail,' remarked Maya.
They were like dogs taken off the leash when Jun told Edgar
and Noel they could finally go into the sea. They should take
advantage of the time while the sun was not high in the sky
yet. He told Edgar and Noel to take Francis along with them.
Jaime said nothing. I hollered to Francis not to go into deep
water. I asked Edgar to watch over Francis or the tide might

carry him off. The three ran off to the water. We were left in the hut on the beach.

Jun and Jaime were at it again when they were kindling fire for lunch. Maya and I had bought the squid we would be grilling from a passing vendor. They were trying to grab the matches from each other to see which of them could make the flame stronger so they could make coals. There was Jaime arguing that they should just use kerosene so the flame wouldn't die out quickly. Then there was Jun reasoning that the squid might taste like kerosene if they did so. They were like that until I almost shouted at them when Jaime forced Francis to swim. Edgar and Noel could swim like fish. 'Francis should watch Edgar,' he said. 'He should imitate what they were doing. Just flap your arms and hands. Kick your feet in the water. Because the sea is salty, the human body naturally floats in it,' he said. I could no longer stand seeing Francis who I was sure had swallowed seawater while flapping his hands in the water. While Jaime was trying to teach Francis, Jun kept calling out to him to just let Francis play with Edgar and Noel. Jun was daring Jaime to follow him into deeper water. It was Maya who shouted for me. She told Jun to stop shouting. I just stormed off in anger. I couldn't scold Jaime because Jun and Maya were there.

Maya followed me to the hut. She said that other kids are simply thrown into the middle of the sea to learn to swim by themselves. I couldn't tell if she was joking or not. I simply laughed. Maya said that when her boys had still been learning to walk, they hit their heads a number of times, fell off here and there. Noel's forehead even had to be stitched up. It was a good thing it healed well so the scar was not so obvious.

Because Edgar was trying to help him walk. Telling him to do as he was doing as though the toddler could understand words at that age. One step first, then the next. Just do as I'm doing. Edgar suddenly let go and Noel fell headlong, hitting his forehead on the concrete floor.

On the way home in the afternoon, everyone was asleep in the car except Jun who was behind the wheel. When we got to the toll gate, while Jun was lining up for the ticket, I saw all the cars in a row, the waiting drivers, the people handing out the tickets from the glassed-in office. I do not know if Jun noticed I was awake as I sat behind Jaime. I noticed how similar people's movements could be. They handed over the payments in the same way. They held the wheel the same way. They leaned back in their seat the same way. The cars were similar. Though they varied a little in colour or design, I could see how they remained alike. A giant machine made up of similar things, of things that were copying each other. I thought that Maya was right. It was not bad. It was not bad to imitate because that was how people learned how to walk, how to swim, how to talk, how to laugh, and perhaps also how to cry. Then I felt a sudden lightness in my body as though a weight had been lifted from my chest. Jun and Jaime were not competing. They were imitating. When we had gone past the toll gate and were entering Manila, I saw just how dark the already dark night in Manila was. Not a single star to be seen in space, making the darkness heavier. So, in the face of the weight of the world, men remain boys, looking for partners, looking for ones to imitate, looking for assurance in the exemplars that like them he can also bear the weight that they are forbidden to pass on to others. When Jaime awoke from the honking of a passing truck, his eyes roamed the darkness. Trying to glimpse where we were. When he saw we were already on the superhighway, he asked Jun if he wanted to be relieved of driving since Jaime had had a nap. I could only smile when Jun readily refused and said he was not sleepy anyway.

6

Smile

Whenever I see people smile even when they are by themselves, I want to ask them what made them smile. Did I have something to do with their smiling? The way I look? Something in the way I move reminds them of something that brings a smile to their face? Or do I have nothing to do with it? A memory really just entered their mind suddenly. It came inexplicably. It was not in the people around them. Not in the music they were hearing. Not in the noises, not in the smells or in the surroundings. Whatever the reason, I still wanted to ask them what had made them smile just like that even if they would be laughed off as fools by those around them.

But I can't ask them just as I can't ask Jaime what was secretly making him smile in the middle of the PTA meeting we were attending with Francis. Was it the enormous earrings of the one seated in front of us that made the ears sag? Even Francis couldn't take his eyes off the pair of earrings that seemed as large as the chandeliers in our kitchen. Perhaps he was simply waiting for the woman's ears to get torn off. Was it the emcee on stage who was out of breath from nervousness in the presence of so many parents? Was it the choir member who could do nothing but smile after squeaking just to finish the song? Was it some parents who seemed to have sprouted eyes in the back of their heads in an effort to gawk at the couple charged with fraud but were there anyway to attend their child's PTA? Was it the mother of a student who is reported to be cheating on her husband with the bachelor teacher of her child who was also there but pretended he didn't know them? Was it the child who was playing with the flower-fabric embroidered onto her mother's chest? The nanny who could barely keep up as she ran after her young wards? Or all of these? I want to know what suddenly made Jaime smile. But I can't ask him. I'd like to share that memory with him. I simply looked at Jaime and returned his smile. I didn't do anything but let him know that I saw him smile and that it was not important for me to know why.

A few days later, I found myself hearing Jaime tell me that he was ready for Francis to have a sibling. We were together in bed, about to sleep. I was surprised by what Jaime said. Even before we had got married, he already told me that he would prefer a small family. Even an only child would be fine by him. So, before we got married, I had already accepted that no one would come after Francis any more. But what was this change of heart now? He who had said that the country's population was already too large, that it was difficult to raise a child in the Philippines. There were so many things to consider, from schooling to medical care to raising the child well amid a chaotic world.

The memory of our vacation was still as clear as our sunburned skin from swimming in the sea. Jaime had been paying for our resort expenses. Maya and I packed up our things before heading home. I saw the boys, Edgar, Noel, and Francis, quietly ogling the ice cream vendor's treats beside them. Jun bought each of them an ice cream cone. He was already eating one ahead of them. The boys were checking out the flavours they would pick. Each one pointing. Each one begging the vendor to add a bit more, as he had put some more in the other's cone. When they all had one each, the vendor left. He was ringing his bell again. Everyone got busy licking before the ice cream melted. Jun simply looked at the three of them. I saw how happy our son was in the company of Edgar and Noel. Jun didn't notice that I saw how he tousled Francis's hair the way he did with Edgar and Noel. He tousled my son's hair when he saw the indescribable smile on Francis's lips when he bought him an ice cream from the vendor.

I could only smile when Jaime said he already wanted to have another child. That night, Jaime became acquainted with the smile he had given me amid the other parents in Francis's school. He didn't ask me any more what it meant. Just as I didn't ask him just the other day what the secret was behind his smiles. There is no response to such smiles except returning them. Hidden things need not be feared after all because everything is hiding a secret. Even happiness.

7

Ritual

Jaime would turn off the light in the room. I'd turn on the bedside lamp. I did not like the dark. I wanted to see him. He would walk over to where I was lying in bed. He would undress as he approached me. The light would play with his body. I'd catch a whiff of his body that had clung to the bed sheet, the blanket, the pillows. The smell was already familiar to me and couldn't be covered up by fabric conditioners. Whenever he would walk toward me, whenever the lamplight would play across his body, the smell would lodge itself in my nose like something new and unfamiliar.

He would join me under the covers. We would grope beneath the blanket. Our eyes, legs, and feet would go blind. I'd feel Jaime's hands on my chest. He would lift my shirt. He would come in as though he was entering a cave. He would unclasp the straps of my bra as though he was picking up obsidian on the beach. I'd grope for the elastic band of his shorts. The hair on his feet would tickle my legs. Our feet would turn into hands while undressing our bodies. His newly washed hair would smell fragrant. As he would enter me, I'd park my tongue there in my sacred space on his body. There in the groove behind his ear that remained sacred to me even though it was no longer just I who knew of it.

I wanted to cast off the blanket wrapped around our entwined bodies. We are not serpents that need to hide in the grass. I wanted to tell Jaime I wanted to see his body above me, beneath me, beside me, with me, there atop the bed that became the sea, undulating, cresting, swaying. I wanted to see how his body became a well of clear sweat, as clear as raindrop, as clear as my tears that flowed in place of blood, but as salty as the sea on my tongue. I wanted to see how his body turned riverine from the beads of sweat coalescing, creating creeks, rushing, creating cataracts, becoming water.

But I couldn't tell him any of that. I could only glimpse his body when the blanket accidentally slipped off as our senses deserted us. When we were regaining our breath. But I wanted to see him from roots to tips, from beginning to end. Perhaps it was truly impossible to wish for such things. Perhaps all of life was not enough to truly know even just one creature. I wished to tell Jaime that I'd like to be his partner in all things. Perhaps there were things I really couldn't tell him, and he to me. There are things that a woman can tell only to another woman. Like I did not tell Jaime the schedule of my check-ups with the gynaecologist. Like that one time when Maya happened to drop by the house.

We chatted for a long time but it was only when she was leaving and we were standing at the gate when she told me that she already wanted to get a tubal ligation. She didn't want to have kids any more. Edgar and Noel were enough.

They might have a hard time raising the children if they were to have more. She said her husband was always in the mood. She even got to joke about it. She said she would tell Jun eventually. Not just that day. She asked me not to tell Jaime or he might tell Jun. Not yet. Someday I might be able to tell Jaime what is on my mind. Perhaps there is truly a time for everything. There are times when only women can meet each other or only men can meet each other. Perhaps someday Jaime can also tell me about him and Jun.

8

Hunch

So when Jaime told me that he would take Jun with him to the Marquesas Islands to look for new designs, I let him. Jaime said that, once upon a time, the Spaniards made it to the Marquesas. They might find some designs there with the natives, according to the historical accounts of the conquistadores. The Spaniards had likened the natives there to the Visayan locals in their tattoos. Jun said he also wanted to see the Marquesas in case he could find a job there. It was the company that would sponsor Jun's trip. Jaime said he might be better off taking Jun along instead of an employee he didn't know and would make Jun his assistant. He would leave me in charge of the house and the factory. He gave so many reasons.

While he was changing clothes in our bedroom, I was packing his clothes into the luggage. I had gotten used to the task, as Jaime had already been abroad several times for various meetings and conferences. I'd simply ask him how many days he would be gone and I'd know how much to pack for him. While arranging his clothes, I would sometimes check up on him as he changed clothes. I'd memorize every shape of his flesh, every curve of his body until they were completely concealed by the layers of clothes fastened by strings, zippers, and buttons. I'd remind myself that Jaime would be gone just for a few days and would come back to me. Upon his return I'd remove every covering on his body like unwrapping a gift. I'd check to see if the body I had memorized on the day my husband left was still there and hadn't changed.

But now, as I was carefully placing his clothes one by one in the luggage, it felt that it was not enough to just memorize his body he was wrapping in clothing. As though it was the last time Jaime was changing clothes in our bedroom and he wouldn't come back. As though there would be none of his clothes left in the cabinet because I was putting them all into his luggage. As though he was leaving for good. I wanted to just pass on the chore of packing his clothes for him. If he was truly leaving for good, he should be the one to do it all without asking me for help.

I was used to not taking him to the airport with Francis in tow. But on that day, I felt anger at not being able to accompany him to the airport. I wanted to banish him right then and tell him never to return. But when he kissed me and Francis before he got into the taxi, I could barely hold back my tears. While I almost dragged Francis away from Jaime as though I wanted to take away his right to our son, I also wanted his kiss to linger on my lips. But my lips remained resolutely pursed. Even though I felt it was our final farewell.

After my husband had left with Jun, I went to see Maya at her house. It was far away. They lived in Rizal. I drove myself. It was a bungalow that Jun and Maya were renting. It was inside what was supposed to be a private subdivision. It looked as though the developer had gone bankrupt and just abandoned the construction of buildings and fences. The houses were small. There was a tiny retail store at every corner I turned. I asked around for Maya's place. I didn't see any drunkards. There were many kids out and about. So many kids. As though all the kids who would have been on the wide streets of our subdivision had all come and packed themselves into the tight roadway here. I slowed down. I was afraid to hit and run over a kid who would suddenly jump from the side of the road. It seemed like I saw all versions of hopscotch sketched on the pavement. My car almost got hit by a ball a couple of times. The children would stop their games at my passing. They would stare at me, trying to see if they would recognize who it was.

Maya was startled on seeing me get out of the car across the street from their house. I arrived just as she was hanging her laundry on the clothes line in front of the house. One end was tied to a star apple tree while the other end was tied to the fence of the lot the house was on. She led me through their gate. Maya let me into their house. She had Edgar and Noel touch the back of my hand to their foreheads. Maya handed something to Edgar and sent him off. I learned later that she had Edgar buy a Coke from the store. I said they should not have bothered. My visit was sudden and I didn't even call ahead. Maya expressed thanks again to Jaime for bringing Jun along to the Marquesas.

But they didn't know if Jun would find any work there. In any case, they said, it was worth a try now that Overseas Filipino Workers have scattered all over the world. Jun was planning to look for someone there who could help him. Instead of forking over tons of money to a placement agency. Jun's dream of working abroad still hadn't died. If Maya were the one to find a job, she would go as well. But only one of them could work abroad. They already had kids, after all.

As I sat in the living room, I asked Maya right away what Jaime and Jun might be doing in that moment. Lest I lose my nerve to discuss the real purpose of my visit. I sent Jaime a text message. I tried to contact him in front of Maya. No answer. 'Maybe they are still outside, going around the hidden isles of the Marquesas that my cell phone couldn't reach,' said Maya. Then I asked Maya if there was anything she noticed about our husbands. I couldn't give a name to what I wanted to ask Maya. I began to take deep breaths. The fragrance of Maya's laundry reached my nose. What should she have noticed about Jun, she asked. I told Maya that since Jun became our driver, something had changed in my husband. He brought us to the beach, he even took Jun with him to the Marquesas. I said I didn't have any ill will toward her and Jun. I was just wondering if our husbands might be in a relationship. 'Probably not,' Maya said to me. I do not know if her answer came more quickly than I had expected. I wanted to confirm if she knew something that she was not telling me. Or perhaps I was merely looking for someone to commiserate with. Perhaps Jaime and Jun really just had a soft spot for each other. Maya asked me if Jaime and I were having marital problems. 'No,' I said. I added that I was surprised when Jaime changed his mind about our having just one child. Maya thought nothing of my concern. Jun was still very sexual with her. That was why she had confided to me that she wanted a ligation. She just couldn't tell Jun who was so fond of Edgar and Noel. But to her, having two kids was already too much for what Jun earned and the income of the one taxi they had someone else driving. She wanted a ligation to make it permanent. She didn't want to rely on the condoms and pills distributed by the health centre of the barangay that was being opposed by the priest in their area. There really were so many kids there, was all I could say to Maya.

I insisted to Maya that Jaime was not like this before. Something was different about him. 'Don't you like it?' Maya inquired of me. And so after worrying these past few days, driving long-distance, and interrupting kids at play, I found myself with the same problem about change.

I who had invented change; I upon whose body change is etched. I thought that perhaps it was not the change in Jaime that was my problem, but the not knowing where it was coming from. I just told Maya that if she wanted, we could start a business. We could keep it a secret from our husbands. In case there were separations, we wouldn't hesitate to part from our husbands. We wouldn't hesitate to turn our backs on them without asking even for a pittance. Even if I were to be proven wrong in my suspicions about Jaime and Jun, there would still be nothing wrong with Maya and me putting up a business. Maya and I would hide our earnings from our respective bank accounts, so that we would have something saved up for when we are in need. Events of life are truly like turning corners, as I wouldn't know what I would come up against until I would make the turn.

I told Maya about the interior design business I had been mulling over for a while. There was nothing more I could do in managing the display centres that were still connected to

Jaime's business. I wanted my own business. Maya could be
my partner. I would take care of the capital investment. We
wouldn't lose money because, even now, every time someone
dropped by Jaime's furniture display centre, they assumed
right away that we were also into interior design. They liked
the way I arranged the store. Sometimes someone made the
mistake of asking for the prices of the décor I had placed in
various corners of the store. It showed on their faces how
disappointed they were that it was just furniture that we sell.
In time, I also started feeling regret whenever I had to answer
inquiries about where I had bought the décor that I had also
worked hard to find.

Maya and I would become business partners. I told her she
could go home to wherever her province was. I'm sure her town
had a product we could use in our business. Perhaps someone in
their town made giant fans or sculptures. Perhaps someone wove
mats or shawls in her village. She could put up a factory of those
products to fill the orders she could get from her own efforts.
She could even help start a livelihood business in her town. If
she did not want that, she could help me look for antique home
accessories. Or look for artisans in glass, wood, steel, and clay,
like the makers of earthen jars in Vigan where Jaime and I had
ended up one time.

I'd ask Maya to accompany me in looking for products
from the provinces that only we, only our business, would
sell in Manila. I'd show her the burnay. I'd ask her if she
agrees with me that it was truly strange that there were still
buyers of earthenware moulded from collapsed vessels.
I'd buy burnay again. I'd place it again in the corner where
Francis had broken what had served as a memento of how
my husband had once helped me.

9

Bad Dream

Are dreams the fruit of a hunch? I do not like what I dreamed about. Not just a dream but a nightmare. A day before my husband and Maya's came home. I dreamt that their airplane crashed. They were on their way back home but their airplane plummeted to the sea. Jaime and Jun did get home but as corpses in coffins.

It was raining when Jaime's plane took off from the Marquesas. The steel body of the airplane was shiny. It gleamed with every flash of lightning across the dark skies. As shiny as the scales of fish in the sea. But the airplane that Jaime and Jun were on was not a fish. I already felt, even from the airport, that it couldn't swim across the rain in the sky. The rain was pouring but the airplane insisted on flying, carrying my husband and Maya's. The pilot probably thought that the rain would disappear as soon as they had flown past the clouds. But it rained across the skies. When the pilot discovered this, they couldn't turn back to the airport because they couldn't see anything. So they continued the crossing of the ocean. The airplane was like a bird whose wings were drenched, which made its steel body even heavier. When they were directly over the sea, the rain intensified.

The waves rose higher. They crested as high as several floors of a building. The tidal wave was trying to reach the airplane that was like a ripe fruit dangling from a tree. Until the sea and the sky became one. All the rushing water turned into a whirlpool. It swallowed the airplane Jaime and Jun were on. Swallowed even the fish and the jellyfish, even the whales and corals. There was no grace now in the way they swam to escape the bait of the raging sea. They were crashing into each other in trying to save themselves. But the whirlpool gorged itself on all the sea life in the salty waters.

I tasted salty tears when I awoke. Why was I pushing Maya to help me keep secrets from our husbands? Why did I ever doubt Jaime? I felt the self-recrimination once again for having placed the earthen jar in the corner where Francis was bound to break it. I can't accept that I have caused everything. I can't accept that it was I, too, who swallowed the airplane carrying Jaime and Maya's husband.

I got out of bed right away. The first thing that came to mind was to call Maya. I'd also let her know. I no longer cared if it would be the two of us worrying. I couldn't bear the weight of the bad dream that visited me. I wanted to wake up from this bad dream I was inside of. The sun was already high in the sky. I had woken up late. Francis had school. I had not prepared his lunch box. Perhaps the maid had prepared it. I hope she had. I hope Francis was already up, showered and dressed for school. I was the one who would take him to school today. Jun was away. I'd just wash my face. Brush my teeth and get dressed to take Francis to school. But when I got to the kitchen, there was nobody there. The plates and glasses were quiet. Even the refrigerator and the dining table. They were all simply there like they didn't care. I wanted to shout at them. I wanted to shout just so there would be noise. Even my feet didn't make any noise on the floor because I had forgotten to put on slippers. No birds singing. No vehicles driving by on the street. No people were moving about. I ran to the maids' quarters. I kept knocking on their door. 'It's already late,' I said, 'get up already.' I almost cried as I called out to the maids. I thought they, too, had disappeared. But they were still there. I felt relieved. They had just gotten up late like me. But they had to cook and get ready for the coming day. They had to cook the rice and water the plants. They had to turn on the TV and pick up at the gate the newspaper that got delivered daily without fail. I still had to wake Francis up. I didn't ask him any more what he had dreamt of. I got him to take a shower right away so he could get dressed for school. While Francis was taking a shower, I called Maya. I didn't even ask her how she was. I didn't ask her any more if I was bothering them. I didn't want to ask any more. I just wanted to talk. I just wanted to tell stories and stories.

HUNCH ACCORDING TO MAYA

1

Washing Clothes

I turned on the faucet right away. Beneath it, the basin of dirty clothes. I soaked the dirty clothes immediately without looking at how soiled each one was. I no longer examine the dirt brought home by every piece of clothing. Dirty clothes are innocent children playing in the street. They go home and confide to their mothers so they will be on their side. They are called dirty so they can be cleaned. Not so they can be listened to and believed. They who are closest to the bodies of people but also the most treacherous. The faucet was almost bursting with water this morning. It would quickly melt away the dirt that clung to the clothes. Next week the water bill would come. Perhaps when Jun would have returned from the Marquesas Islands. Perhaps he would have some money to hand over when he got home. That was where I'd get the money from to pay for the water bill. Whatever money was left would be just enough for our daily expenses. The school was making Edgar and Noel buy all sorts of things. The two have already used up a number of sheets of cartolina paper, art paper, and crayons.

It was early in the morning and Edgar and Noel were already playing again out in the streets. I wondered what game they had thought of this morning: hopscotch and tag. I could see them from my laundry area. What kept me hidden from view on the street were the shrubs of jungle geranium that fill in the gaps in the wooden fence. The day would come when they wouldn't be playing outside the gate. Everything would begin with an invitation to go watch basketball across the street from the town hall. Soon enough they would be the ones playing ball. I wanted our family to leave this place even before our boys grew up. I did not want them to end up like the young men playing ball in the plaza. Their childhood did not last long. They got married right away or ended up in jail for some reason.

'Noel, come over here. Buy me a bar of soap at the corner store.' I called Noel over even though I knew there was still a bar of detergent in the kitchen sink. Better ask him to buy it now rather than later. Our youngest had been indulging in games a little too much. Noel was scratching his head while I handed him the money. He was already learning from his playmates to stomp his feet when told to run an errand. He took the money. He rushed to the store so he could return right away to the game. I wrung the clothes one by one. I squeezed the water that they had absorbed. I made a pile of wet clothes. Separate the whites from the colours. I'd wash the whites first. Mostly Jun's uniform. I'd leave them out in the sun first after soaping them. I wouldn't rinse them yet. I'd put them under the sun first so they could become whiter. That way, I'd save on bleach. They wouldn't be needed soon since Jun was away. No problem even if they didn't dry by this afternoon.

It was a good thing that Jun was able to find the job as Jaime's company driver. Because of that, he was even able to go abroad with Jaime. Perhaps he might even fulfil our dream for him to work abroad. He might finally be able to add more cars to the one he had someone else driving. Rather than he himself having a hard time driving it until it became rickety in a few years.

The kids had paused in their game on the street. They were waiting for Noel. I shouted at them to keep off the street or they might get sideswiped. They wouldn't listen to me. They didn't even turn to look at me. They already knew I was not serious. Cars seldom drove through our neighbourhood. Mostly tricycles. But I still had to warn them. Though they wouldn't listen to me. I was already familiar with the sound of cars passing through our street. I know when Jun's taxi is approaching. The sound of the car had become familiar to me as I waited for Jun to come home after driving the taxi for twenty-four hours. Whenever he was trying to meet a quota because we had bills to pay, I waited for him anxiously because something bad might have happened to him. Perhaps a hold upper on the road. Perhaps someone pulled a gun or a dagger on him. Perhaps he crashed while falling asleep behind the wheel. Perhaps he ended up somewhere far again. Perhaps he was now en route to Tarlac or Nueva Ecija or Bicol. Perhaps he was lost.

All my fears from when Jun used to drive the taxi came back to life. But it was not a taxi he was driving now. I had to forget my former fears. What was taking Noel so long to buy detergent at the store? Perhaps he saw another toy being sold. Or perhaps he stopped to watch a game of billiards or at the arcade. Jun was not here in the country now but in the Marquesas. It was difficult, after all, to banish from the body accustomed anxieties. I remembered that I had nothing more to fear. I already knew what he was doing. No more secrets. I already knew where he was.

I got up from squatting over the laundry in front of the faucet. I went to the kitchen. I picked up the remaining bar of soap there so my hands wouldn't be submerged in water from waiting for Noel. I walked by the mobile phone on the kitchen table. It was charging. Jun had bought me a mobile phone so I could call him during emergencies. The cheap mobile phone he bought had no use right now. He was abroad. I couldn't call him. He had spent on travel clothes. He ended up spending more because he also bought clothes for all of us. He would feel terrible if only he had new clothes. He said he would receive his pay cheque after returning from the Marquesas anyway. Though I was unable to send him a text message or give him a call, I had nothing to worry about because at least I now knew what he was doing. So this job with Jaime is a good thing. He has more time with his family. He was even able to bring us to the beach just last summer. I really should let my body forget my former fears and worries.

I soaped the whites. I made a lot of suds. I rubbed and rubbed. Carefully, I cleaned every inch of the whiteness of the fabric. Noel arrived when I was already halfway through the whites. His playmates were hollering about what took him so long. He was handing over the soap and loose change to me. The basin was overflowing with soap suds. I told him to put the bar of soap beside the mobile phone in the kitchen. The loose change, too. He ran back to his playmates. Before long, they were making a lot of noise playing their game again. I laid out the soapy whites under the sun. I'd rinse them in the afternoon.

I soaped and rinsed the colours next. I emptied the water and suds into the ditch. One by one, the soap suds popped before they vanished. I rinsed the clothes. Emptied the water out onto the ditch. Whatever spilled over the ditch was slowly absorbed by the earth. Moss clung to the concrete that was always damp. It grew on the dirt that I threw on it every day.

The vegetable ferns that had sprouted beside the laundry area beside the ditch were waving in the gentle breeze. They were swaying along with the clothes I had hung on the clothes line in front of our house. It was a fresh breeze that made the ferns and the clothes I had hung sway. I never let weeds grow inside our yard. But I did not uproot the ferns that simply sprouted there. I did not treat them like weeds. I wanted them to grow thicker. I wanted them to broaden their leaves. Let their leaves spread out farther. Multiply themselves. I wanted them someday to cover up the dark ditch behind them that I saw every time I sit there to wash clothes.

I heard the drone of an engine. A car engine. Not Jun's taxi. When I took a peek behind the clothes line, I saw that the children had stopped playing. Edgar and Noel entered the gate. They came to me as I had just finished washing the colours. Uncle Jaime's car was here, my sons told me. So, I was not surprised when I saw Ria smiling at me from the gate.

2

Visit

A glass of Coke was in Ria's hands. She was clinging to the glass as though her life depended on it. She was seated at the very edge of the sofa. I already needed to change the sofa cover. It had become dirty from Edgar and Noel sitting there with unwashed feet. Ria's legs were crossed at the corner of the sofa. She looked like she was praying in the way her hands were clasping the drinking glass. Beads of cold sweat formed on the glass she was holding. The sweat of the glass was dampening Ria's hands.

We were facing each other in the living room. I was seated right across from her. Edgar and Noel had gone out again. I asked them to watch over Ria's car. Many of the kids were ogling at it. It was Edgar I had asked to buy the Coke earlier. I also asked him to buy some ice. Because we had switched off the fridge. We were trying to save money because we had had to spend a lot for Jun's trip. Aside from clothes, Jun bought a large piece of luggage, shoes, and a jacket. The ice cubes in the glass that Ria was holding with both hands had now crumbled into tiny pieces.

She said she had something to ask me. That I shouldn't get mad. She uncrossed her legs, then crossed them again. I felt that this was her reason for coming to visit. Not just a social call. The kids had grown tired of peering into Ria's car. They resumed their game even though the car was still there. Did I not notice anything about our husbands? Did I not notice something about Jun and Jaime? Ria's question was like a pebble she threw into a well. I knew that she wanted to test how deep the well was or if it held any water. Was there something I should have been noticing? I saw the clothes hanging outside dancing in the wind. I felt like I was playing tag with the vehicles while crossing the street. I avoided Ria's question. I was avoiding an accident. She said something had changed in her husband since they hired Jun to be Jaime's driver at the office. Jaime started taking them to the beach. He wanted Francis to have a sibling. Ria was like a child who found a toy. It was just that she didn't know how to play with it. She couldn't even be certain if it was truly a toy she had found.

'Our husbands are having an affair,' Ria said. I couldn't understand her. Her statements didn't add up. Were she and Jaime having marital problems? They were not, she said. 'Same with me and Jun,' I told her. 'If we have a problem, it would be his libido.' That was what she couldn't understand about herself, Ria told me. She didn't know if she liked the change in Jaime because she didn't know where it was coming from. She also couldn't say if she would want to know where it was coming from. I said that perhaps Jaime simply found a confidant in my husband? And for that we were grateful to them for taking care of our family. She was also the one who told me that both of Jaime's parents had passed away, that he didn't have many friends, as he ran their business.

When Ria noticed that she could no longer find any certainty from me, she suddenly shifted gears. Before I knew it, Ria was trying to talk me into setting up our own business. She said she would take care of the capital. She said I could just help her source décor that we would sell to clients wanting renovations and interior decoration for their homes and offices. She wanted me to go to the province and set up a factory to manufacture home and office décor. I didn't tell her I hadn't been to my home town in a long time. I do not even know if they still remember me there. She didn't ask me because she was already so convinced of her own plans. She had forgotten the glass she had been holding. She had set it on the table in front of her so she could motion with her hands.

She said she would take me with her to Vigan. Show me a kind of earthenware that still sells well even though it is the result of a manufacturing defect. She wanted to ask me if I'd also find it interesting. I couldn't understand her because she should have noticed that, all around us, many useless things were bought. If she only knew all the things that I shopped for at the market, which would have been thrown away: the fins, scales, and entrails of fish, the bones and feathers of poultry, the stems of vegetables, the shells of crabs and oysters, even the fur of pigs and cattle. Even pebbles mixed in with grains were paid for by the kilo. Even the murky water that sometimes came out of the tap was paid for, as was the electric current that fluctuated.

I walked her to the gate. Waited for her to get in the car and manoeuvre it out of the narrow alley. The kids who were

playing had forgotten her. When I glanced back at our house,
I saw the laundry on the clothes line out front. Their clean
scent was in the air. I would have responded differently to Ria
had she not chanced upon me like that: my life hanging out
in the open. There were our undergarments. Bras, knickers,
underpants. Patches over arms, chest, legs, privates. Perhaps
she had become at ease with me since our chat at the beach.
She didn't need to ask for permission to drop by for a visit.
I know my husband and she knows hers. Perhaps she just
needed someone to talk to who would tell her that she did
know her own husband.

   Our husbands were having an affair. According to her.
If only she knew. Her husband was not the only one my
husband had an affair with. I know my husband and I could
tell her that it was not only her husband but also many other
men like him that my husband had an affair with. The white
clothes were spread out under the heat of the sun. Most of
them were Jun's uniform. The clothes were weeping as they
hung from the clothes line. They did not deserve to be heard.
It is not tears that can make things clean. It is the bleach that
Noel was sent to buy from the store. The skill of laundering
and rubbing, the spreading out under the sun.

   All secrets end with me. Secrets find their final destination
in me. Later, when the kids go to their respective homes,
their parents will ask them who our visitor was. Even now,
there are whispers in the wind buzzing like big flies. There
are always those giant flies in the gutter. They are even here
in the kitchen. Perching on plates, glasses, spoons, the dining
table. As though they own everything. I do not know where
they come from. Perhaps the flies follow my son whenever
he buys from the corner store. The flies swirl like dust over

there. Sometimes the table on which the pots of food are sitting turn black. Perhaps I'm the one the flies follow from the market. Perhaps they cling to my clothes so they won't get blown by the wind when I ride the tricycle.

I do not know how they can smell food from that distance. There is nothing I can do that can kill them. Not the insecticide. Not swatting them until they die. I even tell Edgar and Noel not to let up on them. But they keep coming back. There are more of them each time they return. They can find the littlest holes in the screen covering the doors and windows of the house. They can return to the spots where there used to be food. The flies have a memory.

Memory insinuates itself into my mind like a fly. The flies had been hovering when a friend told me something about Jun. It was a while ago. Way before we got married. We were at a roadside eatery. There were rumours that Jun was moonlighting by selling his services. Often to men. I asked myself if I'd have been less startled if word had it that most of his clients were women. I could never know for certain any more. Just as I have no way of verifying if I would have been angrier if I were to discover all of it when Jun and I were already married. So it was not just waiting on tables that my fiancé had done for a living. But I didn't care any more. I still married Jun despite the buzzing of the flies around us. They were not related to me. I had no responsibility towards them. I didn't announce in my home town that I got married and now have two children. When I gave birth to Edgar in the hospital, I didn't ask Jun any more where he had got the money, since he never left my side to watch over and care for me.

All secrets end with me because it is still to me that Jun would come home. I didn't tell Jun any more that I already knew all about his jobs even before we got married. I didn't tell Jun any more because I felt that it was no longer important after we got married. I just implored Jun for us to pick a rented home far away from where we used to live. A place where we could start over again. But when we moved to our current home, I found that the big flies were still there. The house had to be kept clean so that fewer flies would get drawn in. If I can't tell Jun what I know, I can't tell Ria all the more. It is still to me that my husband comes home. It is still I whom he seeks for succour. I won't ruin something I have invested in. Whenever he comes home, he never forgets to buy me homecoming gifts and souvenirs.

3

Cleaning

I clean the livelong day. As soon as I get up in the morning, I sweep the yard. I make a pile of the star apple leaves on the ground and make a bonfire of it. After Edgar and Noel have breakfast, I wash clothes while the sun is still low in the sky. Then I clean the house. All the rooms need to be swept every day. The broom needs to get into every nook and cranny, lift and move the tables and chairs to be able to sweep beneath them. I need to sweep away the cobwebs woven by the spiders that seem to be betting with each other on whether I or they will be the first to give up. Before sweeping the floor, I have to wipe down the tops of closets, the jalousies, the cabinets and shelves, even the tables. I have to make all the dust come down to the floor before sweeping all of it out the kitchen door. Otherwise, cleaning the floor will be futile because the dust from above that should be wiped off with a rag earlier will float down to the ground. I do nothing but clean and clean the livelong day.

Because there is so much dust all around. The dust motes swirl up from the street in the wake of a passing tricycle. They swirl whenever a gust gets trapped in our yard. They come into the house on Edgar and Noel's flip flops. They find a way through every crevice in the walls just to invade our house. If I do not sweep them away every day, the cement floor of our house might get covered by the earth from the yard. They would turn muddy in the house. Weeds would sprout under the table, in every corner of the rooms. They would crawl across our wall, ceiling, and roof. Even if I put a rug by the door to wipe our feet, they still find their way in. Even if I put a curtain on all the windows, they still find a way to slip in. But I can't seal the entire house like a tomb in a cemetery.

Dust rules over all. Dirt lords over everything. It is not only the house that I need to clean, even the bodies of my sons, Edgar and Noel. After cleaning the house, I call them in from playing outside so they can bathe. I have to clean every inch of their bodies. I scour the grime from their bodies. I don't leave any dirt untouched, even in their noses, ears, and teeth. I'm never remiss in reminding them not to bring their flip flops into the house, to always wash their hands before touching food, not to stay too long under the sun. So, after bathing, they are not allowed to go out and resume their games. They must stay in the house. Usually, the sun is already high in the sky by the time they have bathed. They are not allowed to sweat. On school days, I take them to school after their bath and pick them up in the afternoon.

And outside, the laundry was not done yet because I was still waiting for the sun to bleach the clothes I had laid out. Only in the late afternoon, when the sun is about to set, would I be able to rinse them. The livelong day I do nothing but wage war against the dirt all around me. I'm cleaning even when it comes to our food. The food needs to be washed. The cooking utensils, the plates, and cutlery have to be washed. Only to wash them again afterwards.

I no longer know how everything will end. Even though I know for sure how the plastic wraps for all sorts of snacks sold in the corner stores end up in our yard. Even though I forbid Edgar and Noel from buying, I still find the plastic wraps in our yard. Even though it is easy for me to tell what caused this or that stain—soy sauce, ketchup, grease, spaghetti, ice cream, butter, etc.—it is still not easy for me to clean them.

And so sometimes it crosses my mind to let things be and just shrug my shoulders. Just let the whole house get dirty, the floor, the closet, the shelves, the plates. Let the roaches and the rats in, the ants and the flies. Let them compete for nesting places in our house. Even a street vagrant manages to live amid all the dirt in his surroundings.

Because of this, I'm impressed with myself for being able to face all the dirt every day. I still manage to get up the next day to wage war against it again. If they are powerful in ruling over their surroundings, it only means that I'm also powerful in cleaning the dirt they scatter in our house. Every day I witness how the newly cleaned places and things get dirty. But I can put up with it all because I also know all the ways to make them clean and tidy again. I know how to make the stink smell good again. To make the grimy immaculate again. To make the rough smooth. How the body feels refreshed.

4

Souvenir

But today, I couldn't feel joy in my house cleaning routine. Because of Ria's sudden arrival, I remembered to clean even my souvenir collection in the cabinet. If she had only called ahead, it wouldn't have been the laundry that she saw. Instead, I could have shown her my souvenir collection in the living room cabinet. I could have cleaned them. Wiped off the dust so she wouldn't sneeze. It was a glass cabinet. The frame was wooden, painted black and designed with white leaves and flowers. Drawings reminiscent of China. But I was not able to show them to Ria because it was embarrassing that it had been a while since I had last cleaned them. I'm now holding a ceramic bell. A wedding souvenir. Two doves were attached to the handle. When I wiped it, the bell made a tinkling sound. Soft, resonant. Not like the telephone that would have rung if only Ria had called to announce her visit.

I thought I'd still wipe the souvenirs because I knew that Ria would return one day. Perhaps she would drop by again without a warning but on that day, I'd be able to show her the entire collection. This kind of visit is the sort that has follow-ups. The kind of visit that gets repeated. Not like the visit to the supplier of candles for baptisms. That would never happen again. A ribbon adorns the candle I'm wiping. I can no longer recall which church the baptism was held in. There are many candles in the cabinet. How many baptisms had I attended as a sponsor? I no longer remember which candle is from which godchild. They only visited me when they were small and still needed gifts. When they have grown, it is only the parents who drop by. I have also stopped going to any of their houses. Same thing with the various debut parties I had gone to. Here are the potpourris of dried flowers wrapped in netting. Here in front of me are the flowers carved into glass. There they all are: fragrant and fragile.

There is a souvenir well made of plaster. Again, I heard how Ria's question had landed. Like a pebble thrown down a well she was trying to fathom. Could it also have been heard by the almost-newlyweds standing under the plastic arch? They were dressed up. The man was in a suit. The woman was in a gown. The woman's hand was hooked into the man's arm. Like they were about to walk toward the altar. There is no reason for me to walk down the altar. There are flies even in the church. There are so many vendors peddling all sorts of things around the church. A dog is licking the spilt tapioca and agar drink on the church's marble floor. The flies are swarming a plastic glass of I do not know what. After the church bell rings, the people will come out and talk simultaneously. The vendors will join in the chatter. There are so many of them that the drone of their patter drifts up to the ceiling of the massive church. There is no point of me hearing all of it. All churches are like that. They do not change. In all of the baptisms, weddings, confirmations, and birthdays I have been to. They become a nest for flies.

Jun's fate and mine are hands clasping each other. Two palms clasped in prayer. Like the ceramic I'm holding. White hands, praying. Cut off only up to the wrist. It is not only I who likes collecting. Jun just doesn't know. We are no different from each other in collecting things. Perhaps this is why he does not object to my hobby. Jun said that he was lucky to land a job as a company driver. I told him it had nothing to do with luck. It all had to do with his collecting clients. Perhaps he had collected those many; it was not impossible to imagine that he would cross paths again with at least one of them. Just like the impossibility of my not seeing any more who had given me the souvenirs. Even if I stop visiting them. Mercy was the name of the one who had introduced Jun to Ria. But Mercy didn't really know my husband. I didn't even know Mercy, who worked as Ria's laundress. Jun was introduced to Ria because a friend of the one who worked in Jaime's furniture factory was a friend of mine. And the friend of my friend was a friend of Mercy's. But he introduced Jun as her friend. Because I was the godmother at the baptism of the friend of my friend who worked in the furniture factory. That was how she found out about the job opening at Ria's. I do not call that luck but investing in friendships, in souvenirs kept in a glass case.

It is difficult to explain to Jun that his and my collecting are no different from each other. Though he might not object to my hobby, he makes fun of it. Because I do not stop at souvenirs in my collecting. Not only memories and friendships. Even kitchen stuff: glasses, cutlery, ladles, basins. Even combs, perfumes, and any items stuck to bars of laundry detergent, bath soaps, and shampoos to entice buyers. Promos. I collect them.

I close the glass cabinet. The rag I am holding is already dust-filled. I go to the kitchen sink to wash it. There is my collection of promo items. There are the dozen drinking glasses I collected from buying peanut butter. There are the three ladles I got from buying laundry detergent. There are the spoons I got from buying bleach. They are all there. I don't laugh at them while I am washing the rag I wiped the souvenirs with in the cabinet. I can't laugh at them because I keep using them. We keep using them in our daily rounds in the kitchen. They do not need to be wiped. They do not gather dust as they sit in a pile in the kitchen.

Luck has nothing to do with my having collected a dozen glasses, and so we are able to drink water, and we have something to wash after meals. Just as luck has nothing to do with my having a friend who also has a friend in Jaime's furniture factory. So how can I tell Jun that I know what he used to do for a living before we got married? How can I ask him if he still does it now, with Jaime. No one can tell whether a person truly changes or not. Perhaps it is no longer important that I get to ask. Because every time Jun comes home to me, he does not forget to bring trinkets for my collection. All secrets end with me, after all. It is in me that secrets find their final destination.

Someday, Jun said, he would buy me dozens of glasses and plates, cutlery, kitchenware that I wouldn't have collected from buying soap. He said he would fill the kitchen shelves with things of the same colour and design. He said he would fill the house with appliances. We would collect songs for the videoke. We would fill the nights with singalongs in the house that we would no longer just be renting. Just like people we know who, upon returning from working abroad, have their own collections of perfumes, TVs, wall carpets, chocolates, wristwatches. The dream to emigrate still hasn't died in Jun. If I were to be asked, it would be enough just to collect taxicabs. If one of us were to go abroad, the other one would have to stay. I'm already collecting children from Jun. Should the day come when we can already afford to buy kitchenware that does not come as promos, perhaps I will still not be able to let go of the glasses and plates I have collected. Even now I can understand the anger I feel whenever Edgar and Noel break a glass or a plate. Jun merely laughs at those because he is still dreaming until now, with us having two kids. Someday, I'm certain that he won't force me in case I do not want to let go of the collections that I have become fond of. Just as I'm certain that Jun and Jaime will remain friends.

Collecting things does weigh on you. In the gradual gathering. I hang the newly washed rag outside. The rag I sewed together from the remnants of old underpants and knickers. Just like the clothes hanging from the clothes line, the rag is shedding tears as it hangs there.

5

Letter

The sun is already high in the sky. I look up at the wall clock. Almost ten o'clock. I have to go to the market. If only we didn't have to conserve electricity, I could stock up on food in the fridge and go to the market just once a week. Edgar and Noel are still out there in the street. I have to call out to them to come inside. I'll put them in charge of the house. Since it is a Saturday, they do nothing but play all day. The two finally come in. Both sweaty from their games. I tell them to take a bath when their sweat has dried. That Edgar would be the one to scrub his younger brother. I can't bathe them any more because I used up all my time in wiping the souvenirs. I have to go to the market.

I take the basket from where it hangs in the kitchen. A plastic bag would be an added expense. Better to bring a bag with me there. Before I forget it, I go to the room and get hold of the letter I'll be mailing to Jun's parents in the province. I'll drop it off at the post office on the way to the market. I wonder how many stamps will be needed. It is Jun's first time sending a letter to his home town after all these years. I fold the envelope in half so I can stuff it in my jeans pocket. I tell Edgar and Noel I am heading out.

I entrust the house to Edgar. Because he is the older one, he will be in charge. I tell them not to play rough or they might break something in the house while I am out. Not to let anyone else into the house. If someone comes looking, tell them I'll be back soon. Edgar nods. He has gotten used to my instructions. Edgar locks the door after I go out the gate. I see how Edgar is no longer a small boy playing in the street when he closes the door as I leave. He is not beside Noel who is already by the window as soon as the door is locked. Already anticipating my return.

'No one would be expecting his letter in the province,' Jun told me. Perhaps there would be no one at home to receive the letter. Perhaps they would all be out working in the fields or out at sea. Jun didn't want to write to them. His parents can't read, after all. They have poor eyesight. 'But they can have his siblings read it out to them,' I say. He still has seven siblings there. Some of them, I am certain, can read. I convinced him to write to his family because there was no one I could send word to in my home town. I grew up with an aunt and uncle. I was young when Mama left to work abroad. I do not remember where. I was left with Papa. It was to him that Mama would send money for my schooling. Papa also looked for his own work. One day, he also went abroad. I do not know if he followed Mama. I also do not know which country he left for. Barely a year after Mama left, Papa entrusted me to my aunt and uncle. Since then, they were the ones who raised me. I do not know why I didn't ask my aunt and uncle which country Mama and Papa had gone to. They stopped sending money when I finished high school. My friends said that perhaps the money didn't really stop coming. Perhaps my aunt and uncle were just not giving it to me. So I decided to leave our place. I'd just work abroad, too. To me, 'abroad' was simply a very big country.

I told Jun that I'd let him go to the Marquesas only if he wrote a letter to his folks. In Jun's mind, he would go to them only when he had become rich. He wouldn't show up for a number of years and would suddenly turn up driving a car. Perhaps he wanted to prove that leaving home had been the right decision. Perhaps he wanted to be a hero to his family. I was certain he simply wanted to fulfil his parents' dream when they sent him to school.

And now, Jun's letter is in my pocket. Just a page of how-are-yous I'll drop off at the post office on the way to the market. So it wouldn't get creased in my pocket, folded in half, I hold it in my hand as I get into a tricycle. I do not want the one page of how-are-yous to get crumpled on the pockmarked road, on the bumps in the street, in the gaping holes from the excavations for electrical lines and water pipes that jack up the prices of commodities. Add to those the petrol fuelling the tricycle I'm on, which always seems to be running after time and always running out of time however desperately it races against time on the pockmarked road that is always a witness to departures because almost everything and everyone leaves. The wheels have grown threadbare from ferrying people who need to go away. More and more petrol is used up for the departures. The asphalt on the road is worn out by the leavings. Even the street names painted on posts at street corners are fading.

The tricycle will let me out in front of the post office so I can drop off the one page of how-are-yous that no one, not even I, is certain will be read. But to my mind, perhaps the important thing is to have something to send, even if it is just a page.

6

Twenty-Five

I see a twenty-five-centavo coin on the ground at the entrance to the market. It has gotten filthy from being stepped on, from being run over by carts carrying produce, fish, meat. I almost couldn't make out its golden sheen. There is a twenty-five-centavo coin on the ground at the entrance to the market, and some kids are playing with loose change just a few metres away. They are making a ruckus as they bet their peso coins that flip into the air as they flick them. The peso coins tumble in the wind before landing on the cement floor, which would send the kids into boisterous laughter, set off their banter. While here at the entrance to the market, there is a twenty-five-centavo coin that has forgotten its once-golden sheen.

It is bad luck to pick up loose change from the street. I don't pick up the twenty-five-centavo coin. Even though I do not believe in luck, unlike Jun. I'm also not disgusted by the mud caking the quarter-coin. I don't pick it up because I can't buy anything with it. If the kids playing with bets were to lose a peso coin, would they regret it? Would they be more disappointed if the peso they lost was their earning from pushing carts? What if they simply received the peso from begging alms, dropped into their waiting palms without the donor even giving them so much as a glance?

I end up beside a woman who is haggling over the price of fish. She calls attention to the pale eyes of the fish, to their lack of firmness to the touch, to the glaze on their scales, even her being a frequent buyer, just so she can get a five-peso discount. Five pesos as heavy as the peso coin I held when I was small. Haggling between vendors and buyers is happening left and right in the market. I score five pesos off, then ten pesos, then twenty pesos. After all, I can't know beforehand how much discount I could clinch at every store. Everything has to be bargained for. I can't be sure where the haggling would end: at one hundred or at fifty? When does the peso have enough value so that it won't be subject to bargaining?

Even betting at the *jueteng* gambling game is haggled for. One can place a bet without having to pay up first. The collector makes his rounds again to take bets for the evening's raffle. The unpardoned five pesos go straight into the collector's pocket without even passing through the vendor's pocket. They even joke that the unpardoned peso will be the one to bring luck. Meanwhile, off to one side, my customary produce vendor is inviting me to a meeting about investing money at a very high interest rate. She says I simply need to recruit five or ten friends to the meeting. It will be this afternoon in the house of Aling Pising, who owns the variety store at our street corner.

The peso coins are flying in the wind. The wind carries them from one hand to another. Very swiftly. Relentlessly. Everything in the surroundings is becoming light. The twenty-five-centavo coins are becoming light so that they drop unnoticed into pockets. The five-peso coins, the ten and twenty are becoming light so they could be used to bet at jueteng. The one hundreds, the thousands are becoming light to become contributions to investments. Everything is becoming lighter and so the prices of commodities are rising. A bundle of moringa and sweet potato tops that one could sweep with before now wilts at the mere whiff of the wind. The basket that one could hardly lift now leaves the market swinging in the wind from its lightness. The plastic bags have shrunk. It no longer takes two people to carry a basket at the market. Only one person is enough. Everything is shrinking so everything is becoming light as a balloon. Everything in the surroundings is becoming light as a balloon, even people's bodies, which is why they can fly out of the country. Even without wings, they can fly after giving away their money. Sometimes their children, siblings, spouses, parents, and relatives are carried off as well. Everything is flying in the wind. Light as spit that spatters amid all the haggling. They all fly as everything in the surroundings becomes light. So why even pick up the twenty-five-centavo coin at the entrance to the market? Perhaps the wind just carried it there. I simply pray that the letter I mailed at the post office would be heavy, even though it is just a page of greetings.

7

Birds

This is why I'll go home to Edgar and Noel while praying for the weight of the letter I mailed at the post office while worrying about the lightness of things at the market in the basket of the things I bought. When Edgar opens the door, I'll see how he sighs in relief as a kid once more after watching over his younger sibling. The wind won't whisk me away, just like the clothes carefully clipped to the clothes line. Clothes that only become lighter, troubled as they dance in the wind, when they run out of tears. I'll collect the clothes in the afternoon before they could get stolen in the dark. But before that, I have to prepare lunch for Edgar and Noel. I need to make them take their nap. I'll wait for the sun to rise to the top and wait for its gradual setting at dusk before I gather the dry clothes and rinse the bleached ones. In the meantime, I'll take a nap along with Edgar and Noel.

Even before my deep sleep takes me into dreams, I'll be awakened by the noise of so many children. Edgar and Noel will have woken up ahead of me again and gone outside to play. Coaxed their playmates to come into our yard canopied by a leafy star apple tree. There they will play until dusk. They will be shouting at the top of their voices as though arguing over a matter of great consequence. They will be as noisy as the birds that rouse me every morning. Horsing around. Chasing after each other. Hopping all over. Not caring if they disturb me in my sleep. Perhaps they mean to waken me so I won't get lost in dreams because bad dreams are most dangerous when they come visiting in the afternoon.

There are so many children in our yard. I no longer know which kid is whose. They are sparrows appearing all of a sudden in the rice fields. As though Edgar and Noel simply fly somewhere and upon returning to our yard, a large flock is already tailing them. No wonder the church and the health centre volunteers have been fighting over them. Indeed, like a pesky flock of sparrows in the rice fields. On the one hand, we parents are invited to attend a seminar about condoms, pills, and other modes of artificial contraception. On the other hand, we get a sermon from the church pulpit about the sanctity of matrimony that should not be violated by any artificial bodily interventions.

On this afternoon, I won't scold Edgar and Noel for playing. I won't force them to come into the house, though the dust may be stirred up in the yard or the leaves of the plants I potted there may be torn. Not on this afternoon because it is their noise that woke me up so I won't be led to dreams. Instead, I'll prepare them a snack. I'll feed them snacks. I'll fry some banana fritters for them. I'll call Noel not to send their playmates home but to have him buy Coke and ice from the store. They will be surprised, I'm certain. Unexpected joys are good. Especially for young boys who are slowly growing up. The joy of serendipity. They would gather around our little table. Gather like birds around a puddle in the middle of the road. A puddle perspired by what used to be a dusty road.

After they eat, we won't wash the glasses right away. We will just pile them in the sink. They will resume playing. I'll go to the laundry area to rinse the bleached whites after bringing in the clothes that have dried from the day's heat. I'll watch the children at play. Sometimes laugh at the same things they laugh at. Like when a kid will trip and accidentally push a playmate into a ditch. I'll watch them while doing the laundry. This afternoon, that is what I'll do because they won't let me be led to some wasteland of bad dreams. Because if they did not awaken me, I know it will be dusk by the time I get up and I won't be able to rinse the bleached clothes. I won't be able to hang them and let them drip-dry so I could bring them in at night, so they won't get stolen in the dark. This afternoon, that is what I'll do.

8

Ritual

I remember Jun before falling asleep. I wonder what he might be doing now. Did he find someone who could help him find work in the Marquesas? Could he be sleeping, too? Could he and Jaime be sleeping side by side? I wonder how my husband sleeps beside another man. I see in my mind's eye how Jaime's chest would be the pillow to his head, just as Jun's chest becomes my pillow when I sleep.

It is such images that lull me to sleep. It is my own hands that awaken me. In the middle of the night. When Edgar and Noel will already be asleep in the next room. They will be snoring, tired from playing all afternoon. My hands will become Jun's hands. They will go exploring the most secret nooks of my body. A spring here. A cave there. A creek to swim in. A sea to wade into. All of them in my body. The blanket covering my body will moult like serpent skin. My body will twist between the soft pillows. The walls will sprout eyes. The moon will enter the room.

It is like that when Jun and I make love in our bed. Always there is a moon rushing to leap over our fence. Entering our yard like a thief. Peeping through a slit in the window at our two bodies twining. And we never stop it from watching. We feel sorry for him, since the moon will never know what this feels like. It is simply there in the sky to watch. To look and look without being allowed to mingle with the ones being looked at. I let it watch me even though I'm by myself with no one but my hands that are Jun's hands. I don't stop it even if it calls upon dogs, cats, rats to listen to my repressed moans. These are moans I let the ears that have sprouted like mushrooms on the walls hear. If only they were real mushrooms, I'd harvest and cook them for breakfast. I'm certain that Edgar and Noel and I would have our fill because of their sheer numbers. I wouldn't have to go to the market in the morning to buy something to cook. I'd simply let them listen to me. I'd feel sorry for them because only I can moan like that, even though I'm by myself with no one but my hands that are Jun's hands as well.

9

Vision

One day before Jaime and Jun were to come home from the Marquesas, the phone in the living room rang. The phone rarely rang when Jun was away travelling somewhere. The phone's ring was louder than the peal of the souvenir bell.

I was having breakfast with Edgar and Noel when the phone rang. They were going to school. The two were eating rolls with fried eggs. Their milk ready in glasses. They tried to hold off on the milk. Both praying I'd simply forget about the milk they had to drink. We were just waiting for them to finish eating the rolls so they could start the forced drinking of the milk. The phone rang even before we could begin to argue, with the two of them conspiring to defeat me.

I stood up to answer the phone. It was Ria at the other end. I couldn't tell if she was sobbing. I could sense the fear in her voice. She said she had just woken up. Because she had a dream. It was a bad dream. When she woke up, fear overcame her that something might have happened to our husbands.

She said she had dreamed of the crash of Jaime and Jun's plane before it could land at the airport. She said she could still feel the spatter of rain all around and how everything was swallowed up. She said she didn't know what to do. She said she would call Jaime and Jun. She didn't know if it was to Jaime or to Jun that she would relay her dream. They might just laugh at her. She said that if she were to tell it to Jaime and Jun, they might switch to another plane and that would be the one to crash after all. She said she had thought twice about telling me, lest it came true. But she couldn't hold back any more or she might burst into tears. She needed someone to tell it to. She asked me not to laugh at her.

I couldn't bring myself to laugh at and dismiss her call, one day before our husbands' homecoming. Before I could reply, before I could think of something that could dispel her disquiet, so that we could both laugh off her dream, before I could even think of all those things, I heard a glass break in the kitchen. Noel froze as he stood there. He was going to pour the milk into the sink while I was not looking. Edgar was trying to stop him when he let go of the glass. He seemed rooted where he was standing. He couldn't bring his hand down as it held on to air where the glass of milk used to be but now lay crushed on the floor. White began to spread over the redness of the floor that was buffed with floor wax.

I had nothing to say to Ria because my heart was suddenly filled with foreboding. I do not believe in good luck or bad luck, but I felt fear from the breaking of a glass, which, come to think of it, was worthless because it just used to be a jar of peanut butter that I had collected.

10

Waiting

The next day, it was only around three o'clock in the afternoon when Ria arrived at our house. She picked me up together with Edgar and Noel. She said we could sleep over at their house tonight. My boys were thrilled. But it made me more apprehensive because it meant Ria had been spooked that badly by her dream. She said she had called her husband on the mobile phone that morning. He said they were fine. It was their final spin around the Marquesas before heading home. He said they had already bought their airplane tickets so they were certain to be home. Jaime had already asked her to pick them up at the airport.

As the time of Jaime and Jun's arrival drew near, Ria's paranoia heightened. She could no longer bear waiting by herself for seven o'clock in the evening before picking me up to go to the airport. She had to do something no matter how early it was. So, she ended up picking up Edgar and Noel and me. We could do nothing in their house but look at how happy our boys were with the PlayStation. They had no clue about their mothers' fears. Edgar and Noel were transfixed by the PlayStation. In the past few days, they couldn't even be tempted to peek into the arcade built near Aling Pising's store.

I saw how Ria looked at everything inside the house: the paintings hanging on the wall, the curtains, the earthenware, the sculptures, the staircase leading up to the bedrooms, the marble floor, the tables, and the chairs. As though Ria was memorizing every detail of the house because they might have changed by the time we got back from the airport.

The helps went on with their work as though nothing was going on. Even though Ria had them prepare supper, she didn't eat. I didn't eat either. I simply said that for sure our husbands wouldn't have had their dinner when they arrived. I'd have dinner with them. We gave Edgar, Noel, and Francis their dinner. We wouldn't take them with us to the airport because their fathers would be arriving late. They might be bringing lots of luggage and they might not all fit in the car. When they had left for the Marquesas, they each took a taxi, and so we didn't know how tight things could be with all of their baggage in one car. We told Edgar, Noel, and Francis to go to bed as soon as we left so that we could wake them up when Jaime and Jun arrived.

While Ria was watching our sons having dinner at the dining table, she was cupping a ceramic glass of warm water. She was having tea. She didn't know where to train her troubled gaze. Tearless but haggard. She wouldn't stop biting her lip, which turned redder. She who only a few days ago had gone to the house to ask me point-blank if I had noticed something going on between our husbands. She who only a few days ago had been convincing me to set up a business with her, decorating homes and offices just so we could have one of our own.

Even now she was blaming herself for why she thought badly of her husband. So what if there was something going on between our husbands, she said. She could accept everything now except her dream coming true. That was when Ria began to feel dear to me. Because at that point we were no different from each other. Even I was biting my lip. I had to stop myself from mentioning what I knew about Jun, and perhaps about her husband, too. But it wouldn't matter if I were to tell her what I knew. Even if the vision of the broken glass in the kitchen were to come true, all the secrets I knew would no longer matter. It is indeed in me that they would find their death.

CODA

1

The road leading to the airport was flooded with light. The lights were bright. The posts from which they hung were all in a row. The car carrying Maya and Ria was entering the airport. The airplane that was carrying their husbands home was arriving. They were picking up Jaime and Jun from their vacation in the Marquesas Islands.

Ria was the one driving. Maya was seated beside her. Ria was very careful navigating the streets of Manila. The urge to get to the airport quickly was struggling against the need to avoid accidents. Even though she knew that arriving early at the airport couldn't make the airplane that would bring Jaime back to Philippine soil arrive any quicker.

The lights were too bright for Ria. Especially when she and Maya had parked the car and they began their wait in the arrival area. She couldn't remember why she preferred the ceiling light in their room to the soft light of the lamp every time she and Jaime made love. Now that she was waiting beside Maya, she would prefer the soft light. The lines of everything she was seeing became sharper. It hurt the eyes.

She wanted to grow drowsy in the gloomy light of candles in a church. She was wondering how restful it must feel to sit in the long wooden pews of a church. She did not feel like waking up even though she knew she was there pacing back and forth in front of Maya.

Jaime and Jun's airplane was arriving at night. So, Maya left Edgar and Noel at Ria's. They would sleep there, in the guest room. Maya had set a nine o'clock curfew in the evening for her sons so they would stop playing with Francis. Ria backed her up and told Francis he had to go to bed early because he still had school the next day. Jun's sons would greet him at Ria's house.

The lights in the arrival area were too bright for Maya, too. They didn't make her squint. But she yearned for the sunlight outdoors. Why was it that Jun's airplane had to arrive at night? The lights in the waiting area were artificial. Reminding her of hospitals. Unlike sunlight that whitens her laundry and dries the water dripping like tears.

They were surrounded by glass. Towering glass. Wide walls of glass. Clear as the drinking glasses collected by Maya and broken by Noel just the other day. Clear as the glass cabinet Maya keeps her souvenirs in. To Ria, clear as the rain, as seawater, and as her tears. The glass does not throw back shadows at them. Revealing whatever is on the other side in its wholeness, concealing nothing. There was a group of lazy people dragging their luggage. Jaime and Jun were not among them. Their flight hadn't arrived yet. But the clarity of the glass was not preventing them from hoping, from looking, from keeping vigil, to try and see if their husbands were already there. The clarity of the glass was fragile. Clear as the drinking glass with ice that Jun had brought to Jaime during their first meeting, as the glass brought to Jaime's lips by the natives of Fatuhiwa whom he didn't find when he went there with Jun. So, they were going home.

Maya glanced at her wristwatch. Ria looked at the flight advisory. Her breath caught. Their husbands' flight was delayed. She told Maya. Her pacing quickened. There was no one she could ask why Jun and Jaime's flight was delayed. Ria's dream was still very clear to her. The sound of the glass broken by her younger son was still very clear to Maya. She saw that Ria's hands were clasped like one of her souvenir figurines. Tonight, her destiny and Ria's would hold hands just like she once thought that her fate and her husband's would be the same.

Maya couldn't smell anything in her surroundings. She had seen the woman beside her apply powder and spray perfume but she still couldn't smell anything. More and more people had joined them in the waiting area but she couldn't smell any of them. Even the hospital smell that the bright lights had reminded her of had vanished. She was careful not to bump into anything. Maya avoided people, tables, dogs. She was afraid that something around her would break. She noticed even the littlest things. She looked at all the faces around her. She wanted to know if they could see she was worried. She was worried that the vision of the broken glass would come true even though she didn't believe in bad luck and good fortune. She felt that everyone around her was looking at her until she no longer cared if it was plain to see she was worried.

Ria was afraid to look at the colour red. She didn't want to see red. The red tail lights of cars were enough, even the red traffic light she saw on their way to the airport. She didn't want to see the colour of blood. She didn't like change even though her body knew blood. Her ear became primed for hearing the cries of the suddenly injured, so she could readily avert her eyes. Ria was sweating. It was not through her eyes that her body's water was seeping out but through her skin. Salty as tears. Why was it that she had that dream. She looked at the faces of everyone around her. There were more and more of them. She was waiting for something to suddenly change in their faces. She was waiting for someone to grow pale or faint, which would mean that an airplane had indeed crashed as she had dreamed.

To Ria, the airplanes parked in the airport were birds. Enormous birds. Gigantic wings. Bodies of steel. She was worried how such heavy things could even fly. Heavy things crash easily. To Maya, an airplane landing buzzed like a giant fly. She didn't care any more. Let all the people talk about her. Let them look at her the way the moon and its companions had peeped at her just a few days ago.

A group of people that exited the airport toward them looked like flies. Maya didn't notice that one of them was her husband. She wouldn't have noticed had Jun not waved at her. When Maya waved back at him, Ria looked at the people who were approaching. She stopped looking at the faces beside her. Jaime was there. Her husband was truly there walking beside Maya's husband. Jaime was smiling at her. Maya and Ria's faces were indescribable as they embraced Jun and Jaime. Their pulses still hadn't slowed down from worrying. And so, they forgot everything they had talked about since Ria had come upon Maya washing clothes. Nothing mattered any more. They could do nothing but ask Jaime and Jun why their flight was delayed.

'It was rainy in Marquesas when we left. We had to wait for the rain to subside. Better to be safe from accidents,' Jaime replied.

'I had broken out in hives from worrying about what might have happened to you both,' Ria added as she clung to her husband.

'We were lucky that we had to wait only thirty minutes. It took the others two hours,' added Jun to Jaime's explanation.

'What souvenir did you buy for me?' Maya asked Jun who put his arm around her.

It was then that they walked out of the airport, toward the car that would take them to their sons who were presently sleeping peacefully.

STORIES OF RENDEZVOUS

1

That was what happened to Jaime and Ria, Jun and Maya. Maya and Ria didn't confess their plans to their husbands. Neither did they attempt to name what it was that transpired between their husbands. Which was why the desire to also have a secret with Maya weighed heavily on Ria.

The next time Ria dropped by Maya's place, she made sure Jun was away driving for Jaime. Ria didn't come across any kids. They were in school. There was no laundry on the clothes line in front of the house. She came upon Maya sweeping the floor. After Maya offered her a seat and something to drink, Maya showed Ria her souvenir collection. Maya opened the glass cabinet. She pointed out to Ria which ones were from baptisms, debuts, weddings, anniversaries, and birthdays. She showed how many of them were of the same design.

'It looks like you have so many godchildren and friends.'

'Some of them are just acquaintances. Friends of friends.'

'You could invite them to work for our business.'

Maya thought that Ria would have lost interest in setting up their business. She thought Ria would have got spooked after dreaming that the airplane their husbands were on had crashed. She thought Ria was just being flippant because of her jealousy. Yet here she was reviving her plans for them. So she spoke what was on her mind. She said that if Ria really wanted to set up a business that Jaime wouldn't find out about, they should not cater to his clients. They would have to set up their business far away from Jaime's furniture business. But it was just that she and Ria couldn't figure out what business they could get into other than interior design.

'What kind of work were you planning to do abroad?'

'Whatever. Perhaps even domestic work. They say the pay is good.'

So, Ria thought that a laundry shop would be their business. It was just right for her and Maya. Though Ria didn't know how to wash clothes, Maya was good at it. Maya knew exactly how to care for clothes. They would start with two large washing machines. That would be their starting capital. Ria would cover all the expenses. Maya would run the business. Ria would take care of the paperwork. Maya would buy the daily supplies of the business. Maya would just have to time it to Jun's departure for work. Ria could already see how they would rent a space in a mall basement. She would talk to the owners of the restaurants and offices into bringing their curtains and tablecloths and other fabrics for washing to their laundromat. They wouldn't need to be there at the shop every day. If Maya would need to be there, she could drop off Edgar and Noel at her house to be with Francis. Ria could already see how her business with Maya could work. They would both keep it from their husbands. It would be her and Maya's secret.

And so Ria and Maya's business took off without the knowledge of Jaime and Jun. Which was why one day, when

Jun mentioned to Maya that he could finally buy a second car for their taxi business, she was happy for Jun without asking him where he got the money. His job driving for Jaime didn't pay much. They were having supper then. Jun added that he was going to hire someone to drive the taxi for them.

'Jaime lent me the money. I'll pay him back in instalments.'

'It is a good thing he gave you a loan.'

'He even said I wouldn't have to pay the interest.'

Maya almost couldn't stop herself from asking her husband point-blank what Jaime's kindness to them would require him to do in return. At least Maya knew why Ria was being nice to her. She just couldn't be certain if Jun really knew what Jaime was expecting of him because it was impossible that he had no expectations of her husband in case there really was nothing going on between them. But because she couldn't ask Jun, she just turned to Ria instead.

'Jaime talked to me last night.'

'What did he say?'

'He wants to expand the furniture business into interior design.'

'I told you that one day he would get into that, too.'

'He wants me to be the one to manage it, Maya. He said he noticed that managing our display centres was not a lot of work for me.'

'I don't understand.'

2

The secrets between the two couples began to pile up until the relations between Jaime and Jun and between Maya and Ria became more complicated. Sometimes, they could no longer understand what it really was that they were keeping from each other. They didn't notice that if they would only ask their children, Edgar, Noel, and Francis, they could easily tell them what had really been going on between their parents.

Like that one time when an ice cream vendor had passed by the front of Ria's house. He was pushing his cart that was painted with images similar to the designs on jeepneys. He was ringing his little bell. Edgar and Noel were stepping out of the gate then. Maya had come to pick them up. It was a Saturday and Maya had dropped off her boys at Ria's. They had just started their business then and Maya had many things she needed to buy for the laundry shop. She still had to manage their employees who were taking care of the laundry. So, when she went to fetch Edgar and Noel from Ria's, she felt a little pinch that perhaps she had been neglecting her children. Perhaps they had gotten spoiled from playing with

Francis. She couldn't even transfer Edgar and Noel to a private school, let alone to the same school as Francis.

So, when Edgar and Noel asked her for money to buy ice cream, she couldn't refuse. As though she needed to make it up to her children. It so happened that Francis had walked them to the gate. Before he could close the gate, he saw Edgar and Noel buying ice cream. He ran to his mother right away. He would also ask for money even though he knew that Ria strongly disliked seeing him buying food from the street.

'Didn't I tell you not to buy from street vendors? It's dirty. You might get sick. I'll just ask Naty to buy ice cream from the grocer's.'

'But she won't be back until later, Ma. The vendor is right outside the gate.'

'Why can't you wait? Do you know how they prepare their ice cream?'

'But Auntie Maya said it's not dirty.'

'When did she say that?'

'They're still there outside. She bought ice cream for Edgar and Noel.'

When Ria went to the gate, Maya and her boys were still there. She could no longer put a stop to Francis's clamour for ice cream. Ria just reminded herself that nothing had happened to her son when Jun had first bought him a street vendor's ice cream when they had gone to the beach. She couldn't stop Maya from giving money to Edgar and Noel to prevent them from buying ice cream. And above all, she couldn't tell Maya that she thought the ice cream was dirty. Ria was not the only one who found herself in such a situation because it was not just Francis who could understand what was going on between their parents. Even his friends Edgar and Noel had once begged Maya to buy them soda from a store.

'That's bad for kids.'

'You had also said that about ice cream from the street vendor.'

'That's different.'

'How so?'

'You've been drinking Coke like it is water. It's addictive. Especially for kids.'

'So why is it that Francis's family always has Coke with meals. He's not an addict.'

Maya couldn't win against her sons' argument. She simply said that it would cost too much to have Coke with every meal. When it came to such talk, Edgar and Noel would have nothing to say. But she couldn't tell Ria that sometimes she thought their lifestyle was extravagant.

And so, at times, it was not to Maya that Edgar and Noel would run. They would turn to their father and give him hints. It was something they couldn't do with Jun, to ask directly for whatever they wanted, something they could only do with their mother.

''Tay, I beat Cis earlier on the PlayStation.'

'Really?'

'Oh yeah, 'Tay, I always win. Cis always loses out to me. Even if he practices the whole day.'

So, when they celebrated Noel's birthday, Jun's gift to him was a PlayStation. Since then, their house became noisy and lively again. Edgar and Noel used to be the ones to go all the way to Ria's. Now, it was Francis who would sometimes come over to play with Edgar and Noel. Whenever they were not in front of the TV, they would be in front of the house. Playing tag or hide and seek with the other kids in Maya's neighbourhood. It was only there that Maya would see Francis become dirty like her boys. She simply let Francis run around with Edgar and Noel. She just made sure that when Ria was about to come get Francis or Jun was about to take him home to their house, the boy would bathe or get cleaned up and change clothes.

When the PlayStation game that Edgar, Francis, and Noel were playing was turned into a movie, the three decided they needed to watch it. They first planned for Edgar and Noel to ask Jun. When their father said yes, they would ask him to get Jaime's permission for Francis to join them. They were certain that Jaime would allow him as long as they were with Jun. But when Edgar and Noel talked to their father, he refused. Their father reasoned that he had work. He couldn't take off just like that. He just said that they might be able to go out the following week. They would ask Jaime if he could work for just half a day. But he really couldn't go out with them that week. Edgar and Noel didn't know what to do. Most likely, the movie they wanted to see wouldn't be showing in the theatres any more in the following week. They had to think of something. The next day, Jaime found Francis knocking on his office door with Edgar and Noel. He didn't understand why it had to be in the office that Francis and his friends wanted to talk to him. It could've been at home. And so, the three boys looked like business partners when they came in while he was seated behind the table where papers continued to pile up incessantly. His children and Jun's were indeed growing up.

'Dad, we just wanted to get your permission. We'd like to borrow the car.'

'What? Why?' Jaime couldn't believe what Francis was saying.

'Our PlayStation game was made into a movie. We're guessing you won't be leaving the office now. Could Uncle Jun go with us? He's just downstairs.'

Jaime couldn't reply to his son right away.

'We were going to ask you to take us, Dad. But Uncle Jun said you are busy.'

Jaime did take a while to respond to Francis, Edgar, and Noel. But when he answered them, it wasn't only Jun who went with them to see the movie. Jaime went along with them too. On the way home, while Jun and Jaime sat in front, the three boys could hardly contain themselves in the back as they argued about who among the characters was the best. And so, because Edgar, Francis, and Noel understood how their parents really were with each other, they could enter each other's world without difficulty.

3

Though Ria and Maya, Jun and Jaime couldn't name the complex relationship of their families, hide as they might behind layers and layers of secrets, their four paths crossed repeatedly, which told them things they couldn't give words to, things they couldn't say to each other's faces.

The corners of corridors are places for collisions. There is no way to tell what is out there as one turns the corner. Even if one walks around such corners every day, one can't avoid being surprised by the person one bumps into. Because it is easy to get used to the hope that the corridor won't betray. That is why at the corner of the corridor, Ria liked sounds. It was the sounds that gave her a warning or a hint of what she might see as she rounded the corner. Which helps her decide whether she should continue walking or simply turn around to avoid the impending encounter.

But Ria didn't expect that sometimes she herself unintentionally would make no noise. So, whoever would be heading to the corner from the other side couldn't hear her. She didn't mean to wear soft slippers one afternoon. It was her birthday then so it didn't seem appropriate to put on leather sandals or any heavy footwear. She wanted everything to feel light on her birthday. So, even before she could turn a corner in their house, she heard two voices conversing. When she became certain it was Jaime and Jun talking on the other side of the hallway, she had already heard them conversing, unaware she was just around the corner. Ria would learn later that Jaime and Jun had planned to wait around the corner to surprise Ria with birthday balloons. But when Jaime surprised her, Jun was no longer there beside him. When she heard Jaime and Jun talking, they were still getting themselves ready. Jun hadn't left yet.

'Do not make a sound.'

'Do you hear someone coming?'

'Is this really okay?'

'Yes, believe me. Maya said that roses are so yesterday. Balloons are the thing now.'

'I wanted to change things up a bit. It's always roses that I give her.'

'And what about me—why have I not received a single rose?'

'Is that a dare?'

'Why not?'

'Leave me alone here. I can do this by myself now. Go to them downstairs. Tell them Ria is coming.'

'I'll surprise you sometime. I'll send it to the office.'

It was not the roses Jun planned to send to Jaime at the office that caught Ria's attention. It was how Jun and Jaime sounded like young suitors as they talked to each other. Two young suitors who were new to courtship so they had to trade techniques. Ria didn't wait any more for Jaime's reply to Jun's plan to send him roses. It was enough for her to know that there really was something going on between her husband and Maya's, without having to rely on a hunch from the little things she observed. She walked back, then proceeded down the hallway with heavier steps but still wearing the soft slippers.

When she turned at the corner, she was still surprised by Jaime. Jun was no longer there. Jaime was holding a bouquet of balloons. The balloons were red, and they felt light in Ria's hand. When she got down to the living room, Francis, Edgar, Noel, Jun, and Maya were waiting along with the help. Francis led the singing of the birthday song. Scattered all around were balloons of every shade of red.

Ria didn't tell Maya any more about what she heard around the corner of the hallway in their house. It was no longer necessary because she and Maya already had their own secret. It was no longer necessary because Maya had also heard this kind of conversation that she hadn't told Ria about. Perhaps when the time came for their husbands to discover their secret, they would also reveal the secret that they knew about their husbands. For now, everything was enough for Maya and Ria.

Maya was the one who took care of delivering the newly washed towels and other laundry items to their spa client in the mall where they were renting space. She was with one of their employees then who was shelving the towels in the spa's supply room. She was waiting for the inventory from the spa's cashier that she would need to make the invoice for the payment collection at the end of the month. She was asked to sit in the customers' lounge.

She was startled to recognize the voices of Jun and Jaime behind the mirror she was leaning on. The frosted mirror was thick, concealing the customers' lockers. She didn't expect that Jun and Jaime would go there for massages. But even before she could get nervous that they might discover her business with Ria when they saw her delivering fresh laundry, she couldn't get up from leaning against the mirror when she heard the conversation between Jun and Jaime behind it.

'Can you get a massage with nothing covering your body?'

'Why not?'

'I'm just uncomfortable because I don't know the therapist.'

'Why, you weren't uncomfortable with me the first time.'

'Well, that was different.'

'What was different with me?'

'You know.'

'That you paid me?'

'That's not what I meant.'

'So what did you mean?'

Maya just heard Jaime saying sorry to her husband. She would have wanted to go to Jun behind the mirror and take him away from that place. Somewhere far, far away. But that would mean having to divulge the secret she had been nurturing with Ria. She heard Jaime's apologies repeatedly. Maya didn't notice her breath becoming deeper. As though she wanted to consume and swallow, to take into her body, the clean scent of the newly washed towels she had just delivered and were ready for use again.

And so, after a few days, when Maya was speaking with Jaime, she couldn't banish from her mind what she had heard at the spa. Ria invited her for a facial and a manicure and pedicure. Maya declined. But Ria was persistent. The kids were in school. They could while away the time at the mall. They could walk around. They would ask Jun to pick them up. Because driving to pick up the boys from their schools would ruin Ria's nail polish. Ria said it was going to be her treat. Maya had no more reason to decline. Ria said she would consider it a huge insult if Maya refused. She said Maya shouldn't feel shy toward her. Why feel shy now when she and Ria were already sharing a secret? Rather than go get a facial and a mani-pedi by herself. Waiting would be a drag.

When it was Jaime who came to fetch them, Maya felt the shame return. She couldn't understand why she would be the one to feel shame when it was Jaime and Jun who were keeping a secret from them. Because she had become privy to the secret of Ria's and her husband's, perhaps she was ashamed of the truth that it was Jaime and Jun who were clueless about her secret with Ria. Perhaps because of the weight of the secrets that she knew they were all carrying for the sake of keeping their respective families together, it felt like she cheated when she accidentally overheard Jaime and Jun's conversation at the spa. Above all, though Maya's load had become lighter by one secret, she could do nothing to help relieve Ria of the same weight she continued to bear. But Maya had no idea that Ria was feeling the same way toward her. That was why Ria had asked her out so they could enjoy themselves just by themselves.

4

Even Jaime was surprised by what he saw when he went to pick up Maya and Ria at the mall. Jun had driven a company guest to the airport. The visitor had insisted that Jaime didn't have to come along. So, Jun was occupied and it was Jaime whom Ria called up next. Jaime was surprised to see his wife and Jun's seated side by side in a salon at the mall. Both women had cotton balls stuffed between their toes. They had their nails coloured.

'How much longer will you be?'

'We're just waiting for our nails to dry,' Ria replied.

'I thought Jun was supposed to pick us up?' Maya wondered.

'I had him drive a client to the airport.'

'What do you think of our nails?'

'It looks like my wife has been turning you into a doll.'

'I even told her, sir, that I might not be able to do any housework any more.'

'Jeez, Maya, have fun every now and then. Get out of your house. You're always at home. That will make you age faster.'

'Pardon this wife of mine, Maya. After all, she has maids who do the housework.'

'If you could only see the help, they look more chic than you. If only I had hair like yours, mine wouldn't be this short. You should come here more often. Next time that will be our project.'

'Jun might make fun of me. All these shenanigans!'

'Laugh at you? You don't want another child after Noel? We shall see. What do you think of my nails, Jaime?'

'I don't know. What should I be thinking?'

'Is it too red or a little pale?'

'You're the expert.'

'Well, I'm asking you.'

'Any colour looks good on your nails.'

'Look at that, Maya, I really don't understand. However much we make fun of these magazines, their tips are still spot-on. Like it says here, Jaime and I are truly compatible. He knows exactly how to answer my questions.'

'What magazine is that?'

'Look at that, Jaime. Could a woman be that beautiful?'

'Why do you even read these things?'

'That's the same thing I said to your wife, sir. Even if she doesn't try, she's already beautiful. I even get to tag along.'

'If you only knew, Maya. Jaime has a home gym. Have you seen it? There's a room at home that's full of gym equipment. So even I end up exercising.'

'But that's a different thing.'

'How so? Tell me.'

'That's for health since we're getting older.'

'Maya, what about your husband, Jun? Does he exercise?'

'His body has always been like that since we first met.'

That was when Jaime realized that his wife and Jun's had become close. He didn't know if he was glad about it or not because that meant their wives might be talking about them a lot. While Ria was settling the bill, he was left alone with Maya. As far as Jaime could remember, it was the first time ever that he and Maya had been alone together. Jaime was worried that perhaps Maya already knew about him and Jun and was just waiting for a chance to tell Ria everything. Here in front of him was Jun's wife and while he was chatting with Maya, he felt that he was taking a test. Maya was the first one to speak.

'I thought Jun didn't go to work because he was busy again with our taxis at the auto shop. Sometimes that's what he does. He doesn't let me know. As though I wouldn't find out.'

'Jun is really hardworking. I don't even notice he still has time for the auto shop.'

'Oh, I haven't had a chance to thank you for giving Jun the loan for his second taxi.'

'Don't worry about it. I just took off the interest.'

'My husband is very happy. It's been his dream to own a couple of taxis.'

'He did tell me that.'

'But watch out, if Jun becomes busy with his taxis, you might lose a driver, sir.'

'It wouldn't be right for him to grow old just driving for Ria and me. Not that I don't like your husband as my driver, mind you. But I said he needs to think of Edgar and Noel. It's a good thing that they're still young.'

'Sometimes it makes me wonder what we might've done to deserve your kindness. Like now, I got a free facial, manicure, and pedicure. These are expensive! In my neighbourhood, all of that would cost only five hundred. Here, oh my, I don't want to ask Ria how much she paid. I just might get spooked by the colour of my nails.'

'Ria is just looking for someone to talk to. Me, too. Jun likes telling stories. Fun to be with.'

'So if ever, you might have a hard time looking for someone to take my husband's place.'

'Why, is he planning to leave us?'

'Oh no, sir. I said if ever.'

'Maybe he's just embarrassed to ask. He can just say it. It would be easy to find another driver. Perhaps he just wants to be a taxi operator full-time.'

'Oh no, really. I said it was just a big if. Jun would be angry with me if he could hear us now.'

'You do know that we don't pay him much. So, I was the one who suggested to Jun to go into business.'

'I don't even know where Jun gets the money to pay for all sorts of things he buys sometimes.'

'Perhaps it's also from his taxi business.'

'It doesn't bring in a lot of income, though. Two taxis? Let's say each one brings in one thousand five hundred. That's already from twenty-four hours of operation.'

'How many is that again?'

'He even bought Edgar and Noel a PlayStation. When I looked in the store, I saw how expensive it was.'

'I'm certain it was the influence of Cis on your boys. Please forgive the kids. Easy for them to want what the other one has.'

'Sometimes I fall to thinking that perhaps Jun has another job. But why would he need to hide it? He can tell me. Why would I get angry? I'm the one who feels ashamed. I told him I should also look for a job.'

Fortunately, Ria had returned from settling the bill before Maya could go on with what she was going to say. Jaime didn't know how to respond to Maya. Suddenly Jaime could breathe easy. He didn't notice he had been holding his breath. But the suspicion that at least Maya knew something about Jun and him had been planted in his mind. The only thing Jaime was certain of was that in case he needed to put an end to his trysts with Jun once more, it wouldn't be like before when he just disappeared all of a sudden. He couldn't just disappear like that. Too many other people were already involved. There were his wife and Jun's. There were Edgar and Noel. They greet them as uncle and auntie as they get in the car. There was Francis who was thrilled to see that he was going home with his playmates. Jaime would mention everything he talked about with Maya the next time he was with Jun.

Jun would also tell him of his own fear. A fear that formed in him when he ran into Ria and Maya at the grocer's. He was shopping for food and drinks and soap and toiletries for Jaime's flat. He suddenly crashed into the cart Ria was pushing. He had no time to hide his grocery items. Everything was there in his cart: Jaime's antiperspirant bath soap that he had started using himself, two kinds of deodorant, one for him and another for Jaime, the toothpaste brand that he had convinced Jaime that they should use in the flat, Jaime's costly shaving cream and his own much cheaper one, a roll of bathroom tissue, a few beer cans, and other grocery items. All there for Ria to see. Jun was even more at a loss when he saw Maya walking toward them. So, his wife and Jaime's were there together, it turned out.

In his panic over how to explain the items in his cart, Jun didn't notice that Ria and Maya were also startled to bump into him in the store. Maya's pace slowed down as she rummaged in her head for an excuse for the sheer quantity of liquid detergent in their cart—not the detergent bars they used at home. A couple of kilogrammes of detergent that she and Ria bought together. Jun spoke up ahead of Ria and Maya.

'Ma'am, that looks like a lot of soap.'

'Oh, I was going to have all the curtains at home washed. Even the sofa covers and bedspreads. It's been a while since we did a general cleaning of the house.'

'I was helping Ria pick the soap.'

'I dragged her along to help me.'

'Are the boys with you?'

'Oh, they're busy with something over at our house, with Francis.'

'Looks like you bought a lot of stuff. Have we run out of soap at home? I didn't notice when I left earlier.'

'Ah, these are for the office. We had run out of supplies in the bathroom. You know, when we're rushing to fill orders, people need to work overtime and sleep over there. I didn't ask them any more what they needed. Jaime said I could just figure it out.'

'You also bought soap for Jaime? This is what he uses at home.'

'Ah, yeah. His soap is different from the one we use.'

'Wait, did my husband give you the money for these?'

'Ah, yeah, because the ones for him cost more.'

'I have been telling Ria that she could save on the cost of soap. I showed her this brand that we use at home. The one at home is just in bar form.'

'Yes, ma'am, that brand is really good.'

'All soaps are the same, aren't they? Sometimes it's just the brand name you're paying for.'

'At least you can be sure of the name. Have you heard the news? Just the other day. Some manufacturers added chalk to the soap they're selling. Imagine that! Those who used it suffered skin allergies.'

'Perhaps those kinds are not sold in a grocer's like this, ma'am.'

'That had better be true, considering their product markups.'

'It seems ten pesos more expensive here, Jun. It's not this much at the store where I buy our groceries.'

'Let's just let things be or we might not end up buying anything because of all our complaining.'

'Ma'am, let me help you and Maya carry those. That's a lot.'

'We are okay, Jun. We will take care of it. There are store employees we can ask. They must get paid well from the prices we pay.'

Still, Jun walked them to the car. He let Ria, who was behind the wheel, drive out of the parking lot first. He tooted his horn in response to Ria's. The two cars parted ways: one headed for Jaime's house, the other for his flat. But Jun drove around among the streets of Manila first before heading to Jaime's flat. And Ria was forced to have the entire house cleaned so Jun wouldn't suspect her lie. Maya felt a great relief that Ria had agreed to go with her to buy the laundry detergent for their business even though it was not part of Ria's responsibilities. Chances were that she wouldn't have been able to explain to Jun why she had bought so much laundry detergent that wasn't even in bars.

5

Jaime and Jun told each other about their encounters with Ria and Maya. They didn't want to add the weight of their fears to their secret affair.

Half of their bodies were soaking in the bathtub of Jaime's flat. In the water they traded the stories of recent days, in the water that made everything buoyant.

Jun was leaning against Jaime's chest. Jaime's arms and hands embraced him from behind. Scattered around the bathroom were lit candles wafting fragrance.

They traded stories of their encounters with Maya and Ria. Jaime and Jun told each other stories without asking any questions.

They just left the speculation about what would happen when Ria and Maya finally found out about them at the bathroom's green door, which was ajar.

Even the leather shoes parked by the door of the flat were asking if Jun would remain just a driver even before they got worn out.

Had his desire to fly abroad died? the ceiling light that was turned off asked the light of the candles that were laid out on the bathroom floor.

Would he not have regrets in case he fails as a taxi operator? added the blind TV to the query of the ceiling light.

If Jun leaves, how hard would it be for Jaime to let go? was the blue question of the heavy curtain that didn't let even a single ray of sunlight into the room.

What about their kids and wives who have become each other's friends? continued the carpet that absorbed all the noise that feet make.

Would they be able to find other men in their lives? What about in their old age? Would they not tire of each other? rattled off the row of bottles of perfume, aftershave, cologne, and lotion that looked like little soldiers standing guard in front of the mirror.

Would they lose their desire for each other when all their secrets were revealed? How could they say that they truly loved each other? quietly asked the cool draft of the air con inside the room.

It was dark, cool, and quiet in the room that was teeming with questions.

In the bathroom, Jaime and Jun were talking about their wives but the only question they allowed themselves was about housecleaning.

'Did Ria really have the entire house cleaned in the past few days?' asked Jun.

'Yes, why?' replied Jaime.

Inside the room the bed remained very quiet. Even the bedspread, the blankets and pillows on top of it. They were harbouring questions that couldn't be uttered even by the socks that were folded like a dog in a corner, by the trousers and shirts that were feeling the strain from being draped over the backs of chairs.

Does Jaime ever think, whenever he is on top of Jun, that here is a man like him, an enemy that should be beaten in all things, here beneath him as someone conquered by his triumph?

Does Jun ever think, whenever he is on top of Jaime, that here is someone benefiting from society who has brought him all his misfortune, here beneath him and ruled by him?

These were questions not even mentioned by the secretive bed in the middle of the dark, cool, and quiet room. Concealed even by the bedspread, blankets, and pillows on top of it.

And because they were questions not even mentioned by the secretive bed in the middle of the dark, cool, and quiet room, they didn't shatter along with the other questions when, from the bathroom, Jun and Jaime suddenly laughed with the ambient candlelight glazing their wet bodies.

6

At that moment, Ria and Maya were also laughing. They were inside a coffee shop at the mall. They were relaxing after a visit to their laundry shop before heading home and picking up their kids from school. But no one could hear their laughter that remained cooped up inside them.

They were playing a matching memory game with their bodies. Ria was no longer afraid of the colour red. Maya was also no longer afraid of breakable glass. They no longer noticed the comings and goings of people, whispering to one another like flies. Their table had become like an island for them. Ria was sipping coffee while perusing a magazine. In front of Maya was a glass of soda and she was content simply watching Ria reading.

Ria's hand that was holding a teaspoon was having second thoughts. Would the sugar be good with her coffee?

Maya would lean back in her chair. Would red lips go with white porcelain?

Ria would rest the teaspoon on the lip of the saucer. Maya would look over at her. She couldn't decide if silence and having company were truly compatible.

Ria would turn the pages of the magazine she was reading. She also couldn't decide if conversation and reading went together.

'Might Jun have mentioned to Jaime that he saw us buying very many packs of laundry detergent?'

Ria looked over at Maya who had leaned forward in her seat again. Should she cross her left leg over her right, or the right over the left?

'I even had the entire house cleaned just to be sure.'

Maya gathered her long black hair. Her fingers tucked some wayward wisps behind her ears.

Ria noticed that Maya's short nails were just right for her long hair.

Ria touched her own hair and uttered a prayer that her eyes would match her short hair.

Ria's red nails went with everything, including the magazine she was holding.

Do wet lips really go well with a moist glass?

How about red and wet lips? How about a brown hand on fair skin? A pale hand on a brown leg?

The two of them were certain of only one thing. Hot coffee suddenly spilled on the table between them wouldn't do.

When Maya handed Ria the tissue, her hands said that she could love the woman now sitting across the table from her.

When Ria took the tissue from Maya, her fingers that brushed against the mound of Maya's palm expressed the same feeling.

It was then that the laughter of Ria and Maya exploded all around them. They laughed and laughed until all the people around kept looking at them at their table that had become an island for them.

In that moment, they felt how the weight of all the secrets they were carrying became light. Their laughter was enough to lighten the load of the secrets they bore. Jun and Jaime's laughter in the bathroom was enough. Ria and Maya's laughter at the table was enough. It was enough for Jaime so that having accidents in his life could remain a ritual. It was enough for Ria so that she wouldn't be confused again by the riddle of the red rose. It was enough for Jun because it was his right now to enjoy good luck after the series of misfortunes in his clan's history. It was enough for Maya to have a collection of three children and four parents, four friends and four lovers. For now, everything was enough for them to live as one family.

Acknowledgements

I dedicate this publication to the memory of Randy Bustamante for believing in this novel and translating it into English. Thank you to Joey Bustamante for trusting me with Randy's translation. I would also like to thank Karina Bolasco, Christian Benitez, and Julian Dela Cerna for their guidance in seeing this novel through publication.

Thank you to Melvin Mora for his invaluable support while I was writing this novel.

This novel was translated from the original Filipino, *Sambahin ang Katawan*, which received the NCCA Writers' Prize in 2005. Thank you to Edgar Calabia Samar for publishing the original Filipino in *Tapat: Journal ng Bagong Nobelang Filipino*.

And, of course, thank you to Nora Nazerene Abu Bakar, and the entire Penguin Random House SEA for believing in this work.